OS5 GRIND SYNDICATE
PART 3
B S BHAMRA

Os5 grind

syndicate

Preface

Th idea came to again when I ws having a beer I was
staring at the empty bottle of beer thinking that I would
like to travel to the place of where the bottle of beer
was made and making a story of this.

The bottle of beer was a bottle of ale the destination
was to go up north I personally at this moment was not
in the position to travel there but however writing this
story had made up my mind to stay put. I do not know
if you knew that I have a disease called schizophrenia I
am a writer.

I hope that one day that I will be able to complete this
journey as for now ill just write about it it is just as
exciting.

Os5 grind

syndicate

Introduction

This is the third part of the os5 grind syndicate quite
similar to the frost and second and Benjamin is in
trouble yet a again once. With Lucy in control and
Benjamin as usual acting cool however still her ginning
pig. With Benjamin thinking about two things one to
escapes and two to stay put and do the experiment.
With Lucy taking him through his mind place to place
as they look for the microchip which is supposedly to
be hidden some place in Benjamin. As for lucy who s
teams of scientists had made a machine that would
control benjamins mind as he enters it to find the wear
abouts of the microchip.

CHAPTER 1

Benjamin awakes still half asleep scrambles to the bathroom and is sick, realising that he was late for his meeting that was going to change his life. Benjamin ahs a contract to sign one that would secure him finically well in to his future. Benjmain was thinking first as he is a little bit late he has his meeting at the hospital not only was he a student in science. He was putting himself forwards to be put into an experiment he ws going to be a gerbil he ws going to be tested on.

Benjamin did not acre at that point he just wanted the money simply to fund his studies he has no parents and he ws already in debt he does not have to many friends either however the money that they were talking about seemed extremely adequate. If everything goes ok he would be finically secure for the rest of his life. With in the next two tears he would have enough money to pay his student debts. Enough to finish his studies.

The company that were looking for students, clients, the experiment was 0s5 known to most scientists as the grind syndicate.
After having a seriously long thought Benjamin gets all the details and is making all the right moves Benjamin is on his phone. After giving them his details and statistics he fitted in perfectly the colour of his eyes his weight what he eats to the colour of his hair everything about him ws now being recorded.

Even though Benjamin thought what he was doing was exciting he did not know what he had just signed himself in for. Within a couple of weeks he would know there ws one way in and know way out.

Benjamin did not know this signing the contract in angst and not treading it at all. However he ws excited as he outs his contract down aside. Into his student bin in his student accommodation in his bedroom he was feeling good.

He had kept it to himself for a long time in act he did not even tell his teachers or any other students friends not that he had s]any at that time.
Benjamin is thinking that it was great idea covering his finances it was simple he was just going to use it and ague it in the experiments it would be fine pop a couple of pills Benjamin has no idea and gets paid for it. Benjamin thinks it was going to be a laugh little did he know.

It could not look any better through Benjamins mind he keeps it to himself he says nothing to anybody as he lays on his bed dreaming of what he was going to do with al of the money.

Benjamin is at his desk waiting for the phone call he is just finishing his last essay and dissention on the spirit and the mind of the body arriving of the phycology. Benjamin was clearly talented and how often he had boasted and laughed about the subject he had taken. Benjamin was still waiting for a phone call from the science labs he was in California the labatory's were in sanfrancisco as Benjamin finally given his instructions and he plans to make the journey within the next few days.

He has to wait for some paper work and it would arrive the very next day. As excited as Benjamin as waking up quickly and in some kind of shock as he gets out of bed and greeting his postman which was unusual. As Benjamin watches him the postman posts his letters this was happening everyday for the next few weeks Benjamin ahd an obsession he even once got to follow him and got caught and was sent away the post man even threated him as he was following him closely, to closely. On one occasion Benjamin was right behind him like a devil.

As Benjamin watches him as he posts his letters they are well a where that he ws there, Benjamin did not know that he to was being watched. Benjamin is watching as he mail that he wanted was or had not arrived and Benjamin was left watching other students getting there s.

Benjamin on this occasion get s Let down there were letters but no letters for him there ws nothing in the mail box for him. The large blue letter box lets Benjamin down again it was empty again for another day.

Benjamin was in a sulk not totally upset but upset enough and feeling a little down he looks around he says nothing as he dips his head in shame and embarrassment.

A couple of days latter Benjamin receives a letter the letter was one of acceptance it ws the lettr that he had been waiting for.
Benjamin was looking t the letter s there is a knock on his door. Benjamin can hear an argument close by. Which says everything about his student accommodation as he continued to read the letter ignoring the knock on his door he continues to read the letter which is inviting him in to the veracity in the desert.

Benjamin is delighted he already knows that he was enjoying the experiment, it was right up his street. And as unusual it would suit his mind as for the gain of knowledge that would be a bonus Benjamin was already up for learning new things.

What Benjamin did not know that he could walk in but never walk out. And as for the contact tat he had signed a few of his details had been changed just to suit their laws.

The letter received had a time and date on it and Benjamin and Benjamin knew that he would have to leave the college for a few days they did not care they did not give Benjamin any time to prepare himself for the journey and new everything was now rushed booking the ticket form the train station from the college was a nightmare even more so the ride to the train station it was the hardest thing he had done al week.

Anyhow with Benjamin finishing hs last sentences on his dissention that he was writing as he finally puts his pen down looking at what he had written and thinks that his work was done and was good. As Benjamin congratulates himself again as Benjamin runs down his corridor in excitement bumping in his rooms mates telling them that he was too busy to talk right then. Finally ending up out side right in front of the tutors office. To tell them the good news what his plans were as he hands over his last dissertation.

Benjamin does not wait around as he has a coach to catch, Benjamin hands his work over it is in a large white envelope and it looked and felt heavy, it was to heavy Benjamin s easy was not as short as you would think.

As he puts his work in an envelope on to his tutors desk not stopping and coming back out of the office and there was other students coming in to the office fast as Benjamin leaves he was gone he was off. the summer time had just arrived and Benjamin was on time.

Benjamin awakes again as he awakes realizing what he had just experienced was a dream it was not real. Un expected and disgruntled by the whole situation the experience realizes that he was going to be late again.

Benjamin grabs a quick wash in and by he is sink he gets dressed neatly as he is on his way to the last lesson of the year.
Not forgetting the letter the invitation to the os5 grind syndicate which had not arrived yet. Benjmain leaves his student accommodation and he is on his way to class. Benjamin was late for a meeting that would change the shape of his life.

Benjamin did not care at that point he just wanted the money to pay for his studies. As Benjamin is late for class as he moves running through the corridor's towards his classroom which was a large room amphitheatre only to get lost and has to continue looking wit no idea or sense of direction. As Benjamin comes to the last door at the end of the corridors hoping that he had found the room enters it.

As he greets his teacher by not saying nothing but making sure that he was seen as he takes his seat. There are lots of excuse me on benjmain side as he try's to find his seat.

As Benjamin casually takes his seat the teacher now fully disturbed by benjamins appearance shouts you boy sit down. then the teacher changes his mind and polity asks Benjamín to leave the room.
Benjamin looks at him hard then realizes that he was not being welcomed and has to leave the room.

Benjamin says nothing as the room erupts with converstion just of r a few seconds. Benjamin had truly been embarrass, as the class room cheers Benjamin is a standing close outs ode listening to the class.

Benjmain misses the last lesson of the year, as Benjamin awakes again it was another dream Benjamin rolls over on to his other side and still not at peace still semi conscious falls back to sleep and again he dreams.

The os5 were watching him carefully Benjamin does not know where he is and the os5 team where considering awaking him. Simply waiting for him to awake. It had been along long time and they were taking ij to account the dangers of waking him up could be.

Benjamin does not awake at that point however while having hs mind and body sleeping and dreaming while the images of his dreams could be seen.
Benjamin was wired up the os5 grind syndicate were in control and they were looking for some thing. In Benjamins mind they could not make it any clearer than that.

Benjamin continued to dream while being watched and monitored. Benjamin is dreaming and this time it looked like he was on the run from something or somebody.

As benjamins heart rate is running fats faster then his mind twice as fast as normal, the scientists at the veracity the os5 veracity the syndicate was looking at him closely in disbelief they think that some thing or Benjamins mind has caught on. The argument was tat he was a sleep. And what could you do in your sleep. It looked like Benjamin had found some thing.

Unfortunately it was not what the scientists were looking for it was an accident something past down form gene ration to generation it was disregarded sat that moment. However it was the topic of the conversation for te next few weeks. According to benjmain he had been an ancient warrior some time way back in the past many years before benjmain was going to be improved of this was soon as he wakes. That meant that he was actually quite cool. There was something cool about Benjamin.

Benjamin was founding out that his mind had a history. It could be that Benjamin was doing the things the right way his mind had a pattern to it. There was some kind of evidence that genetically and where now I question I benjamins mind Benjamin has an actual history.
Could this be that the way that Benjamin was thinking and today he does things a patten of his symptoms inherited and sat down form generation to generation. The os5 grind syndicate were on benjmain the os5 were happy with what they ahd found.

However this was not the reason that they were using Benjamin the os5 grind syndicate were looking for some thing different it was something that Benjamin said, spoke about whilst in conversation a few months ago as he was signing his papers the contract.

Benjamin was unsure of what he had said he was asleep now and was being watch as the os5 want him to say it again. Unsure of what he had d=said had left him in this position.

CHAPTER 2

It was time to move benjmain needed a change of sea
nary was at hand, and then applied very quickly still
Benjamin did not awake this ws neither the time as al
they anted ws deep and in Benjamin's mind. They were
still looking.

Benjamin was moved again and again until he looked
comfortable it would be very soon that he would be
woken up
Only to be questioned about where his mind had been
every dream every thought everything tat he
experienced and everything he saw within hs mind.
And anything else within him.

As Benjamin is still sleeping the science team are
concerned he had been in their for a quite a long time
they were considering cutting the cord Turing off the
machines Benjamin was not in one of his position
Benjamin was alone it was his decision it was the
situation and if Benjamin was to find out where he was
even though he would of told the truth he would still
have to hand it over to him.

Benjamin did not know that they had a plan for him and
it would be put in it's place after they had received the
microchip. Benjamin does not know yet that he is

carrying it inside of him inside the memory inside of his mind.

Some how Benjamins agrees to being given himself up he did not realise that he was being set up right from the start there was no money and their ws no0 fast cars and their was no women no photo shoot nothing. Their was no fame. As for the dream s they did not exist they were just their to keep Benjamins thinking about the micro chip which was stuck in side of him. He was warned about his situation and about the position that he was in.

Even so the science team could of seen exactly the same as Benjamin it was lucky that nobody had noticed what Benjamin was actually doing in the images that were being transferred from his mind in his sleep to them into the screen before them all to see.

Before Benjamin awakes he is on the run from something scary he did not have to be told for the some strange reason his mind had told him he knew that he was in danger.

It was true as the science team retrieved the money from the envelope they would remove him this was Benjamin's own thought. He did not trust them they were os5 grind syndicate. Nobody did.

However not knowing himself Benjamin he had hidden the truth further into and to the very back of his mind and his thoughts. Benjamin asleep was playing tit cool. As the science team watch him as he sleeps contemplating waking him up simply for answers and ton see if anything had changed maybe a result.

Still Benjamins is dreaming and more images were being shown in front of everybody on the screen in font of him. Sill Benjamin is sleeping not aware of the images tat he was sending them for everybody ton view. Still asleep not knowing what he was going to experience next Benjamins mind knows where it is however the images and Benjamin were fighting it was like that Benjamin did not wat them to find what they were looking for. He did not want them to find it.

Benjamins connection to his brain and his mind was too different subjects all together his brain would control his mind not vice versa or the other way around. Benjamin was pushing it hard to keep the images that everybody was watching abbey the os5 grind syndicate were watching they wanted Benjamin nice and awake however it looked like Benjamin was clever enough to tell himself to hide the images as he thought of it was done.

At the end of that evening the science team decided to quite they could not find it after several months of Benjamins sleep and benjmain could not wait to be awoken. All Benjamin had to do now was to serve the after effects and side effects. The only to other things that Benjamin had to wait for was 1that he would be locked inside of quarantine and he of course had to survive his awakening.

Lucy was still out of town however simply looking for the results of Benjamins awaking and there little experiments that she was controlling.

Benjamin said he was looking forwards to meeting her again it seemed like it had been years in fact it was only a few months well seven in fact. They both ahd changed the weather was very good and everybody had noticed t6he trees were not so green anymore and te ground was feeling softer and the weather in general was taking its toll on the earth as when it was going to rain according to the clouds. It looked like summer was not on its way there was a dep g-feeling about tat comment around the lavatory's.

It looked lie the seasons were in season a season to soon. Some thig had changed. The sun was out and the reverses was happening. However the sky's looked the same as always it looked like got Benjamin that the summer was two months ahead of its self they were a few seasons early. As for everything thing in the grounds the leaves on the trees had blossomed months ahead of its self.

Benjamin is set in two worlds the real world and the world of the planets destruction he knows that he is welding something so small its powerful a millions time more powerful as a thought nothing physical just a made up thought which was slowly becoming real. He had told nobody yet and the medical team where still looking for it in and thought his mind.

He was tempted for the first time tom play it cool. Benjamin asked them not to remove the micro chip however they came to a solution quickly and it was only a idea and it was to make a copy of the microchip the item in question benjmain could not find it.

After a lot of looking and thinking and the conversations the science teams think that benjmain was crazy he had lost it he had lost his mind. They start a debate and question it themselves.

So Benjamin thinks that it was possible that what he ws welding and what they were looking for could actually exist in two world s benjmain us put back to sleep and which he sleeps until he will retrieve the microchip but a photogenetic version a carbon copy of what he thinks is the microchip is from inside of his mind and body.

That's what the science tests said if tats the case ill
draw up the contract. It would be a plus ill let lucy
know and bring him back in soon
What did he ask for this time? just as te science team
was about to answer their boss walks in it is "Lucy".
"Hay Lucy ".
"Lucy".
"Good afternoon Lucy".
"OK stop the bull crap Benjamin he already knows why
he is here let go lets find the microchip".

Benjamin is looking at his newly formed position he get
in and gets out as soon as possible if it was possible.
"Hay lucy". Benjamin calls her over to him she does
not move as she stands there waiting for Benjamin to
continue his conversation. Lucy still has feeling for
Benjmain walks up towards him with a polite smile on
her face.
"Hay Benjamin". Your back for some more".
Benjamin answer her. " well schools out I need
something to do and as I received the invitation how
could I go with out seeing your pretty face".
Lucy replied. " bull crap what s the real treason that you
are here".
"I just thought I would make up the penny's".

"Yeah ok well I hope you enjoy the ride ill make it as smooth as possible".
Lucy's words were slowly offending Benjamin he continues. " it is Lucy is it not".
Yes it is lucy. Benjamin continued " Well I will have nothing to worry about will I".

" You think you're so clever coming back things have changed I have changed its not like the other times its not that I am not at the top anymore the big boys are InControl now benjmain they make all of the discussions so keep your head down and keep your mouth shut".

Benjamin was looking at his newly formed position he a thinking that he should get in and get out as soon as possible.
" Hay Lucy" Benjamin calls over to her. Lucy still had feeling for Benjamin she walks up to him with a half polite smile on his face.

Hay Benjamin your back for some more benjmain
answers her well college is out I needed some thing to
do and as I have required this information how could I
denied your pretty face.

" Hay Benjamin bull crap what s the realo reason that
you're here. " Like you said what's the real reason that
you are here. Benjamin is questioned again. He finally
answers. Erh just to make up for some penny's"
" yw=each well good I hope you enjoy the ride. Il make
it as smooth as possible and as painless as possible.
Those words form Lucy were ofending Benjamin he
continues. " it is Lucy is it not"
"Yes it is". Benjamin continues well I will have nothing
to worry about then will I",

You think that your so clever coming back things have
changed benjmain
As Lucy wakes up she was dreaming of that
conversation which she had had a few hours before as
he snaps out of it as Benjamin walks in to her office.
Ahh the day dreamer Benjamin compliments her Lucy
has an attitude as it is Lucy is now on the receiving end.

Of her business as she is called in to her bosses office which ws once hers benjmain from a distance can see what's she is taking about it looked lie, Lucy was taking blocking and as there argument continued there voices could be heard from behind the glass window of the office. They could just about be heard not just by Benjamin but everybody else in the surroundings area.

It was about Benjamin and when he had heard his name he was motivated to shout and join in to the argument only because he could hear them and clearly see that a Lucy a in trouble.
Lucy's boss was on top of her mind he ws on Lucy's case it was not going to be long before her boss to had now began to shout to the point of things over towards Benjamin but who had clearly done nothing but shouted back in his defence.

After he had heard his name mentioned more than a few times. Lucy's boss wanted to be introduced to Benjamin as he leave she office and approaches the large machine that Benjamin is strapped in side of it how ever she is upside down and pointing up wards.

Benjamin is in control to play with its controls of the machine at that point nobody was stupid enough to give anybody else the control of the machine control of some thing that Benjamin created through his mind with Lucy by his side.

Lucy's boss steps between Lucy and Benjamin and the machine, as Lucy boss in traduces himself to Benjamin, they have never met and this was both of there first encounter. The boss in produces himself as his boss Benjamins being none of the wiser greets him polity and that was it the boss had no questions to ask him and no greeting of encouragement.

To Benjamin not continue the experiment Benjamin was surprised as lucy was too knowing how the conversation was going to go she kept her mouth shut and kept her job. Benjamin still knew and was disconcerted by his position.

Benjamin was already used to his surroundings he had been told by the science team that he knew where he was and he knew his surrounding s well.

Well enough to escape however benjmain had put himself in time on this occasion time wa non longer running no walking through and across the desert as for the punishments for hs actions.

Benjamin knew that he would have to stay however he had just finished signing the contract s realizing now it was an mistake he should of read the small print. When Benjamin wakes up from his slight situation tht he thinks that he is in he starts to crack up not that he ws already totally insane in the first place. However it was only for a few minutes and as he re gather s his mind and thoughts keeping them away form lucy.

Lucy on the other side of things is a little disappointed with the os5 grind syndicate they were taking over everything and even more so the experiments the project and it looked like benjmain and lucy were both going to lose.

Lucy was trying to explain to benjmain and he ws really not interested he did not care all he was interested in ws the money the super large pay check at the end of this.

If the worst came to the worst he would do a runner knowing that he would be caught made it more super fiscal tat he should try at least once.

He remind s Lucy again of what had happened the last time they had met, lucy changes the subject as it looked like there was a change in the wither. This slowed things down Benjamin was left alone with nothing but a storm to listen to.

It was not so like benjmain to go walking off especially if he had been told to stay put. There were some restrictions about his movements Benjamin was not told why yet.

Benjamin was standing up watching lucy they both were watching the storm and =especially as they both wait for the flashes of the ,lightening and then with the sound of the thunderous thunder. Which rocked the veracity and echoed loudly above them. As some of the lights went out only to come back on a few second s later.

As the storm comes to the end the sound of the rain just stopping and a little pitta patters of droplets slowly hit the floor hard enough to still be heard by Benjamin and probably the other around him.

The large gust s of the wind still smashing loudly against the windows they were tough and unpaintable Benjamin was happy to be on the right side of them Benjamin notices the number on the door he had been there before. As the rain stops and disappeared and there was nothing left to watch with just the od puddle left flowing gently by the curb side downward towards the drains.

CHAPTER 3

After the rainstorm had dried up Benjamin was free to roam around again however it was not to far as he was locked up in his cell. And once again felt awkward.

Benjamin was feeling hungry he would normally call the restaurant down stairs with his orders it was built into the veracity however instated he goes off for a walk in to the veracity to find out where he was ordering the food from only to find out that it is the os5 grind syndicates restaurants. The place ws filled with futuristic cops benjmain was not welcome.

It was clear to him at that moment that he was going to pick a fight a verbal fight one of many words and o-ne that he would never forget. Everybody in the canteen joined in however Benjamin was very with some answers them every time he ahd answered them.

It came up to the point of quite a lot of police men and cyber police women and actually stopped eating to listen to them both argue some of them tried to join in.

Benjamin was at battle of his wits quickly finding answers to all of the questions tat he ws being asked as he answer s every question polity and quickly until the words where gone silences nothing no words another silents as benjmain ahd come to the end pf his conversation. Nothing came out of his mouth.

Benjamin was standi9ng tall like he had accomplished some thing as he places his order. In fact he then changes his mind and leaves a few dollars on the counter. Benjamin walks out with a bag taken form the canteen cooker chips burger and a soft drink. As to Benjamins uprise there was silence as he walked back across and through the police as he made it to the students door. Looking at the entry sign with a lot of relief.
As he moves coolly and smoothly back out of therest8urant saying nothing not speaking as he sucks through the straw on his milkshake.

As Benjamin is making his way back to his bedroom he bumps in to Lucy they meet each other and have another conversation about the experiment. Once again Benjamin is getting it in his neck. It was funny Benjamin was just thinking about her. As he says it too her is it true that the whole plan hates me or is it me I always seem to be on the receiving end and for the same reason.

What's going on Lucy butts "in excuse me your
wanted In the lab". as he points his finger and
continues " your meal". Lucy snatches the bag of chips
then the whole half of the burger right out of Benjamins
food bag.

Benjamin says nothing lucy takes another bite handing
it back to him.

Benjamin signs with disappointment and asks which
direction were they heading in lucy points and then says
to him " That way." Benjamín nods in agreement lucy
stares at him prompting him to go.

As Benjamin is taking another slap to his face for his
mistake and follows Lucy's instructions.
Lucy is watching lucy carefully benjmain knew thi9s
and he thinks that three are different versions of Lucy
and he thinks he has seen them all three of them. The

first time was out side of his bed room window he said that he could hear her breathing she was close right next too him.. and then a again closed just out side close through some glass window then one patio with closed doors.

But which one ws benjmain believing was the real one Benjamin was asking himself these questions as he is interrupted by video call on his monitor and goes what Benjamin say as lucy the real lucy males her request that she would like to see him up stairs.

Benjamin bed room door opens automatically controlled by a switch upstairs Benjamin compliments her as he gets of his bed there were doors everywhere the space they had was inappropriate and junk Benjamin thinks that he could sneak around them as they were all electronic in fact the doors were not audible and they were silence when they opened and closed.

Benjamin decides to run and hide as he is the target he is o the run first of all the small street inside of os5 as it is in the middle of the desert and then around the corner I to a building

It looked large enough to his in side of it. The os5 where hunting him as they emerge around one of there street corners benjmain is forced to change his direction and hides again whilst he hides he is spotted by the high security cameras this time they defiantly see him. he makes another move and again he is clear of the danger te os5.

Benjamin leaps up in front from behind the parked cars near by. Not one but from three chnagi9ng his direction again heading back up the street past some smaller buildings. Benjamin is getting desperate he is trying each door he comes to ll the doors so far are locked shut and tight. The so called os5 grind syndicate were homing in they were getting close r and closer to him. They were right behind him they were that close Benjamin dose not give in as he tries the last door in the block of buildings he pushes the door and it opens Benjamin walks in casually. Only to her the sound of a car engine close by out side they had found him again.

Benjamin still does not give in he makes sure that he would make a run for it. This up the street towards some taller larger buildings it all looks to familiar as if benjmain had been there before and he had. Probably on one of his dreams. Benjamin stops he is thinking.

As he round up to smoother building he tries the door he is in luck again.

Benjmain does not want to disturb anybody or hurt anybody or endanger anybody else he refuses to knock on the door instead he notices aa large metal fence at each side of the house benjmain is thinking that he could climb over them, if there were no dogs on the other side he could actually escape.

There was none benjamins was in and in luck too. Benjamin makes a move over the top the large black gates resembling the large doors to w with mans estate. In to another garden to Benjamin surprise it was a smaller garden than he thought.

He takes a god look around and within a few ,minutes he had unlocked a padlock to a motor cycle it was a shame as the bike had no fuel in it it could have been a good way pf escaping.

However his luck had not run out just yet on this occasion, as he attempts to open the larger gates in front

of him although this did not have to much of effect a
Benjamin was just about to be caught Benjamin had
been found.

Still Benjamin make another move over the larger gates
then a fence and again. However Benjamin did not
know that he had been found and was being followed
although he gets all the help that was needed via a
bench that was left close by a bench which he would
use to climb over another fence and up a wall in to a
bath room through a building and in to an empty car
park.

Benjamin looked puzzled as for what he had achieved
after his large effort for an escape he had no idea where

he was as the desert was behind him and he could see little further than car park.

That was where the thought was coming from that he had been there before and it reassembled tat he had been shot io9n that car park many years ago Benjamin was thinking that there was a conversation and that's why he had chosen to be there. His reaccusing dreams and to the fact that he had been there before it was like looking at your own grave stone. Benjamin had fallen in to ahis past again

Benjamin is running and does not stop until he finds a group of people, benjmain dis concerned with his surroundings strips off clothing his clothes in to a near by bush a place where you would always s find astry clothes. As he kindly asks some passer by for some help only to be ignored.

Benjmain was busy making up excuses about his clothes in hope of getting somebody to help him. As Benjamin continued asking for help and as for having no clothes he was looking rather serious.

As Benjamin is still looking for the answer to get himself dressed he could se that the public where not to interested in given Benjamin the help.

Benjamin is getting the wrong idea his own paranoia kicks in he is now twice in danger Benjamin un dressed and cold as he is running out of ideas he can hear people laughing and talking close by him it sounded like the crowed that he had just left.

And the crowd that he had just left behind was now in a an ark wards position as he was now un clothed and streaking.

It was not too soon that the os5 police arrived they had finally caught up with Benjamin as Benjamin was arrested as Benjamin is desperately trying to explain but nobody was listening. And then when he mention the os5 grind syndicate the police take a bow and cut to his bosses.

Benjamin had still not figured it out. The police had made the call and benjmain within the hour was back inside the os5 grind syndicate varsity.
However it was not the end of Benjamin attempts to escape he did it again once more in fact twice he even had people video of it on there phones he was seen spotted ina café having a cup of coffee they were not sure if it ws him but it had great awareness. They only found out it was him a few weeks later. They were fined. Foer with holding knowledge.

Benjmain needed to leave he was feeling no better the=an the day that he walked in to the place and as for the medication he goes out side of a walk and with all the excitement of thinking about of he could scale the walls. And with all the drugs that have been pumped in to his body he might ,lose his way o the journey.

The airport was not the smallest of places and it as a a place that was made so you could explore and as Benjamin had got himself lost whilst dreaming of escaping.

Once he had found himself and found himself back and as for avoiding any of the police and local thugs and the local authority's Benjamin clumsily loses his wallet leaving him with nothing to prove his identity.

You would think that he would panic however it was the opposite as he runs his hands down his sides and pockets feeling his way inn to his clothes and feeling hard for what he refuses to believe that he had lost.

He finds nothing as the wallet was gone. The next feeling after was an automatic one he would try and think about where he had been and think about the place where he could of left it. He has no ideas as for tracing back his steps all the way back to the café. "No" Benjamins says to himself. " the phone booth no" the man that tap me on my shoulder". he continued. "No he was to close I would of felt him
 " for the cigarette no, the man on the other side of the bench".

" I have been pick pocketed and he must have been a good one."
Benjmain knows with out no money and with out it he would have no money to fly. Game over he ws on his way back to the os5.

Whom incidentally were close by watching him as well as following him. As soon as it was clear they would make a move as soon as Benjamin has left the air port he was kidnapped bag over his head, forced In to the back of a van driven back to the desert an sent back to lucy in the vercility and back in to Lucy's experiment.

As Benjamin had travelled far a few hundred miles and with out any money because he had lost his wallet at the air port.

Benjamin had got as far as holland before the os5 G syndicate had caught up with him.
And for being on the run it was not helping but helping very little.

Benjamin heads for the busiest place possible, it was going to be the airport again Benjamin knows that he is running out of time they would find him he was well aware of this because that is what they did.

Benjamin had scrounged a few pounds enough for a bus ticket he was now doing it that way. Benjamin upset about being in the position that he was in and was board of carry his medication takes it all. Hoping that his plane would land quickly this played a big part in Benjamin mind his next move towards his escape was getting closer.

Benjamin was dressed casually and in disguised out of the old normal ruff stuff in to nice jeans t shorts and pumps and of course a shirt with matching socks just so he would blend in lie the caterpillars that he was he often thought why. He was now fit enough to enter the air port it would be impossible to find him unless the security cameras would pick him up
And if all of that makes sense Benjamin is on the run. As Benjamin was watching the os5 he was watching them a little to close as he noticed something that he did not noy=tice before the os5 that were right i9n front of benjmain not just fully armed but were carrying these super large knifes the kind of knife an ancience warrior would be carrying benjmain unostentatiously understood that message he knew what they were for.

It was basically a back up it went with the uniform there was no ritual with it. There knifes were of sacred instrument it was only used and drawn in self defence. For a few minutes benjmain wanted one it would make him feel none the safer though.

It was just some thing to talk about to himself for a while he continued to talk and watch them until he noticed another thing as a verbal argument occurs. One of the os5 catch Benjamin eyeing up his knife however

Benjamin was quick in complimenting him and moving his eyes away form his hip he removed his eyes from the police mans piece.

There was another officer standing close by he understood smiling at first then jokes letting everybody know and there was some laughter to follow.

CHAPTER 4

After another brief conversation and confrontation Benjamin leave s the officer, the refilled room heading downwards towards a corridor which was also headlong downwards towards the experiment room.
Benjamin stops looking at his creation straight from his mind the machine. That monsters was going be taking him back in to the past and even more so in to the future. Through his mind I suppose you could call it time travel.

He still does not understand it fully with out the os5 grind syndicate scientists none of what Benjamin had created would of happened. They did not care what they did they were just taking orders. Neither lucy thought to much about them in fact she thought they were quite rude.

Even more so to much thanking and caring could leave you, With Benjamin it was different it was just an act on behalf, the questions was Benjamin stupid enough to fall for false kind ness from Lucy's whole system.

After standing for aa good half an hour Benjamin is at a loss not knowing weather he should attempt to go in side of the laboratory or simply continue back to his room. Either way Benjamin felt disappointed that it ahd Sayed with him for the next few hours Benjamin was now dreaming of doing another bunk.

Benjamin is back in his room on his bed he falls asleep. Almost insatiably he is dreaming and towards the end of his dreams he is dreaming of his neighbours however it was not related to the vercility or the os5 or even Lucy. It would have been more normal if he was dreaming of his family instead. He was dreaming of the 0s5b grind syndicate.
And the odd dreams of past arguments
Benjamins dreams were not so good they were more like a series of night mares however on this occasion he is dreaming of past conversations. And different situations all about the same things except for one thing they all ended differently. Right to the end everything else in the dreams were the same. What benjmain was going through was a hard thing to do.

Benjamin fails to understand them it was like he was fighting in his sleep fighting himself fighting the dreams

The mind in question being constantly asked question the same questions and other over by the scientist and to top it all off benjmain knows and he is reminded as it all is being recorded.

Once again Benjamins mind is else where he is thinking about other things like escaping he was finding the thought quite a frill. He was going to attempt to steel some of the files that thought takes him way back Benjamin starts to reminisce. He remembers thinking about this a few weeks ago back then it was just a thought benjmain did not think that he would think of it again and again and again.

It had come to the time that Benjamin needed questioning and he was not particularly convinced or wishing to take part he was not as you would put in the right frame of mind.

The company the os5 grind syndicate were asking the questions instead of Lucy who was nearby.
 A few things had changed since Benjamin had been there the last time. Lucy was no longer in charge and the g syndicate were in full control of everything including the experiment lucy was way down the stats she was back at the bottom of everything the company does.

Even though Benjamin needed questioning as for the wear abouts of the microchip they wanted to know if Benjamin was ready. Ready to go off looking in side of his mind for the microchip. The minute thing that everybody seemed to crave after. It was becoming the topic of conversation in the office Benjamin clear could not handle it with out Lucy by his side and walks out. He ws left to do so he was left to his own devices.

Benjamin explains that he was not feeling like himself all Benjamin could say was that the microchip was a small very small dot on a piece of paper hidden in side of himself in his mind it looked as Benjamin explains like a bar code but over a thousand times smaller microscopic.
When he explains this to the os5 g teams they look at Benjamin in disgrace as they think that he had lied to them. They believed that he was hiding it.

Benjamin asks for a drink it was just to much information looking upward and finally agreeing ton himself ta t he had one for the first time.

Benjamin was lost and in two worlds and literary in two frames of mind.

Benjamin was lost in two worlds he could hear the dogs coming loud barking they were talking about him. Nobody else nobody apart from him understood apart from him.. tat was a good sign that nature was him that was part of his life.

Benjamin was thinking darker thoughts he head been left alone benjmain awakes quickly after a good sleep and a few days dreaming Benjamins walks upon a bus he thinks that he has missed his stop. He thought again for a second time thinking that he was early and the bus stop was a head of him.

As he arrived he was thinking about the people this life this mind he was thinking about the girl behind him the girl would not stop talking about him. As Benjamin continued to continue his journey.

At that point benjmain was taking it like a man he wanted to get drunk and he did it was simple that it was his life.

Benjamin under he influence had left himself in a vulnerable position this was not known as Benjamin is on his mind he was changing his thoughts his mind in a sense he was thinking in a different way on a level. As Benjamin thought of the experience and the experiment Lucy was having a few knew ideas as she knew no different for a few days. Until she ws told.

And when she heard about Benjamin s behaviour and the news of him experimenting she lost her temper and flipped.

Two days later lucy has her team by her side an was confronting the oos5 grind syndicate.
In the office she did not have the answers they were all looking for and thinking about it was probably a good idea.

Benjamin realises and prefers to be in his room he is content he was congratulating Lucy as for what she ahd done.

After a break in the communication Benjamin is in no better position than where he was from in the first place and as for his temper as Benjamin thinks he is guided he believes and even more so get even more angry . Benjamin finds himself in an really difficult position as he struggles to keep his mind.

Benjamin was back to his usual self he was back in his room at his desk he was watching the weather from his window he did this a lot and a lot of the time he was transfixed.

What the problem was not actually a problem was that there was no rain but the clouds always said that their was a storm on its way the could was different and according to the book that lucy was stuck in they had different makes Benjamin was impressed.

Benjamin was going to chose himself a name and once he had done this he created a new person within himself.

Benjamin closes his eyes once more not focused on anything in particular he was in danger he did not know as he struggles to keep his mind. The team up stairs did not understand benjmain was suffering by ignorance each time he confronted as he felt confrontational towards them as they knew no different as he has to explain himself only to mis understood but still he was expected to ex[plain.

What and why and how to them in a language that they could understand in language that Benjamin did not know.

They were all playing the game they were playing the game of not understanding and misunderstanding. At this point Benjamin knew very little. However he understood.

Benjamin was trying to figure out what kind of contract that he had signed. With a blank expression on his face there's a knock at his cell bed room door Benjamin in a mood already does not answer it. For a while anyway as the person behind the door was not giving up. In fact it shouted while asking to speak with him.

Benjamin feels presumed and finally grows up and opens the door. Una sure of what he ws doing and what was behind the door and when he finally feels like it he needed some body just about realising opens the door to nobody.

It looked like Benjamin ahd missed the call.

As he shuts the door again believing that somebody was there and it was not his mind playing games with him. Benjamin looks upwards to the camera which ws place neatly above him up on the bedroom wall. He knew it was there,. He looks up on it hard with the expression o9n his face was looking a little discontent. As if he ws shy when in fact he was quite the opposite.

As he continues to stare up to the camera just looking at it hoping to get the attention of the person on the other side of it. Which was normally Lucy. Lucy catches on he needed a change of scenery she is thinking for Benjamin as Benjamin thoughts could be heard. She is thinking about how she could help Benjamin and with that thought decides to invite him back up stairs again Benjamin was privilege again. He was there for the rest of the day.

Benjamin gets to sit in the chair in the machine that his mind created it was a special chair and a good experience it was going to be used in the experiment.

Lucy did not know yet but that was a mistake not a big one but one that she would never forget.
As Lucy and Benjamin talked about thi9ngs personal things and the experiment. As Lucy comes tom the end of Benjamin's topic at tat time for the conversation.. lucy slips up telling him not to press any of the buttons on the chairs panel Benjamin catches on. As he calmy says which ones this one he says pushing the button. Which was one of seven and seven being the one that he had pressed.

A big mistake in Benjamin mind he had just turned on the chair. The chair has many functions and mechanical functions it moved back wards and forwards it was like a toy and it answered only to Benjamins mind at that point. Benjamin does not know how to control it yet. Meantime Lucy had not noticed what Benjamin had done. He did he had switched the chair on.

That was to come later as benjmain was being thrown about trying to buckle up. As he is being thrown about

in the chair lucky it was not out of the chair as it had
started to spin.

Meantime lucy still had not noticed and was calling up
her team to the laboratory Lucy catches on all she could
shout to him was to buckle up she was cool in situation
theses things happen all the time when she is a round.
She shouts too benjmain again to buckle up.

As lucy shouts again excited ly buckle up you huckle
berry your going in to your mind. Theses were her
words before benjmain was to far away with the
machine he ws up in the air lucy had no chance in
reaching him. Lucy knew how to switch it off it was
just if Benjamin could hear her. Lucy shouts to him the
coinvents to switch the machine off.
Before benjmain actually goes in to his mind. Lucy was
recording the whole thing on a tape recorder exactly
what was happening and what they both were
experiencing .

For her notes as she speaks in to a totally different style
like she was some kind of scientist which she was her
normal voice locked back in her mind it was all funky
stuff like. The being is on it's way to you huckle berry
is going to move the wizard has a woken and other little
saying only lucy knew what she was saying as it was

all encrypted and only she understood what exactly what she had said.

It was done in a way that would protect her self and Benjamin in the future. It was their to stop the members of her science team stealing the ideas and selling them on it could happen
Lucy has her own personal codes. Lucy was now shouting to Benjamin the words hit the button still Benjamin did not hear her clearly enough and in doing so goes in to the mind and in to the future as the machine was set to go in to the future.

Benjamin awakes in a cold field it looked like to Benjamin to Benjamin and Lucy teams that Benjamin experiment had started early.
Lucy's only real worry was Benjamin and lucy hoping tat he would be clever enough to bring himself back he had no knowledge of how to use the machine.

While Benjamin was exploring his new world in his mind lucy was making phone calls to the os5 grind syndicate to come up stairs to retrieve him.

Lucy's next words were something the lines where something like I hope Benjamin plays ball I can see things getting worse.

CHAPTER 5

Benjamin was left a lone he was still asleep after the experience in and wit the machine and his mind he only meant to sit in the chair lucy has to explain as she does protecting Benjamin not knowing what the consequences were going to be it actually took him in to the future and their was a possible chance that they may have disturbed the future.

As Benjamin's awakes not knowing where he is he appearances the first obstacle his mind. His first thought was that he was back at os5 and was in his cell. Because it was a cell that he was in. it was not a police cell it was the medical unit in the os5 in the future, he thinks.

Benjamin looks around feeling norsiush and then he was actually sick in a small bathroom in the cell. He splashes some water on his face the room that he had just walked out of the bathroom looked larger than he first thought and once back in to the cell bedroom the same happened again the room looked larger.

Benjamin was think fast and thinking of excepting that the fact was that he had not realized his position he was still in the building in the os5 f]grind syndicate.

After a few more times being sick he had totally felt and ws feeling clam the little shock as for his arrival had surpassed. Band again his recollection of how he had got in to the position that he ws in was going through his mind and how fast Lucy had found him as well as his team Lucy had got Benjamins back.

Benjamin choose s to relax he throws himself on to his bed this was a little mistake of pushing a couple of button s on the machine which he had made.

Lucy is the first to approach him Benjamin was not to welcoming after pushing her off him a couple of times she gets the message he complains. " What the hell are you doing". Get off aha-gain were his words.

Even thorough Benjamin ws being ignored the experiment went on it continued this time with a different result even though benjmain he was a lab rat for now and he knew that lucy knew.
Benjamin closes his eyes waiting for the a results only getting them wrong Benjamin was sane he was out side watching the crowd of people walking past him.
Benjmain gulps thinking again of the escape route this time their ws not one.

He knows it would be practically impossible however he knows that it could be an impossible attempt rather than just impossible. As he had tried it before. Benjamin was leaning across and on the table in front of him the tears were in his eyes he was struggling and needed help he is in a mess.

Benjamin is watching the weather again he is still thinking about the escape he was watching everything.

CHAPTER

6

Benjamin wanted timescale he was fed up with the whole situation and the experiment as for being locked up and in and out of his mind Benjamin was making phone calls until he is caught.

As there are no phones in the veracity any more new rules according to Lucy as when Benjamin asks why he has no signal. And to top it off when the words nobody gets out once they get in made Benjamin think twice about his position.

Benjamin was thinking and he was thinking hard and at that very moment he had thought was he would use the machine to escape combined with his mind kept it was not going to be easy he had a good chance.

With the machine attached to his mind it would be a better idea if he should just run.
Benjamin is pacing up and then down in his cell room past his bed and looking up at the cameras watching him. He had totally forget that he was being watched only then to realise he picks up an towel and throws the towel upwards on to the camera blocking the view on the other side. There was a second camera however it was out of reach.

This did not worry Benjamin to much or even bother Benjamin the slightest this only encouraged Benjamin to do it more often. He would do the same again leaving the os5 no choice. As for Benjamin he was busy he was making an attempt he was trying to pull it off if he could breach the walls he was just out of reach he ws disappointed as he failed.

Not knowing if he had been seen or not as he continued only to give in he completely gives in only to force the team upstairs to come down stairs to pick up the pieces they move quickly to Benjamins cell. And he is questioned about his behaviour.

Benjamin is always ready for a verbal disagreement. He really enjoyed a good argument he enjoyed the whole process the winding up and everything else that came with it. Once again once done the os5 free Benjamin he was free again to roam around the os5 vercility Benjamin chose to stay put in his cell after Benjamin had given them a mouth full of filth he gets laid in to that ws nothing to worry about he was used to it. Mean while being pushed around and let himself being bullied Benjamin lifts the guards keys first part of Benjamins plan done it had been put in to place. The second part was on its way.

Benjamin has a big smile on his face as he cleverly hides the keys from and both of the cameras And knowing that nobody would approach his room again with out him in it.

Making trouble leave's them in the dark out side in the lock of a closed door stepping out to remove them when Benjamin in fact should be returning them. Shortly after.

The keys were not just for his door they also opened other door s up stairs to the science labs it would be a busy place up there. Benjamin already knew this. Benjamin was welcome he liked to cause trouble just to tease the science team. As it was his designs that they were working on not for him but for lucy and the os5 grind syndicate. He was on his toes when he was up stairs.

And once sure of his position he returns the keys back to lucy nobody said anything or saw him as they were to busy. Benjamin was wishing that he had kept them and he said to himself consciously tat if he could remove them once he could remove them again.

Benjamin really believed that.

It had been some fun for that day all on Lucy however Lucy was not happy being played about with weather it was benjmain or her anybody else including her new boss. It was through the mind she was and the difference was that she was qualified with what she does Benjamin was not.

Benjamin hands the keys to her the cell keys ton her with a big smile on his face wiping the smiles from her Lucy had ton call security

Lucy did not lose her temper completely just for a small moment well she was shouting at Benjamin for a bout five minutes Benjamin realises that she was a very serious person her words were something along the lines of which one of you had lost there keys. Benjamin was surprised as he thought that they were Lucy's which explains why the science team where following

Benjamin around. You fool lucy continued. You get in my office she says then changes her mind you get out of n=my office. Benjamin was close by listening and finding it funny. There guards that where closest to her were all relived form their duty's.

They had made a big cock up. Lucy shouts ten days come back then. Her boss was none the surprised as he heard the whole conversation form away off. Lucy was now busy being side tracked as she dishes out double shifts basically to let Benjamin know that she meant business her guards were neither less impressed Benjamin ahd looked to of done them all up.

Benjamin knew he was close to getting out except there was one thing he was having second thoughts the place had actually grown on him mind you he was none the patience his thoughts raced about him he ws not patience enough he was always in two frames of mind.

As Benjamin has not been sent neck to his cell he is busy looking at the mind machine as he runs his hands down it sliver sides an speaking to it like it was a baby lucy close by listening .

This he was saying was a cool piece of scientist equipment Benjamin compliments it and then reply's that it works in return. Benjamin ducks underneath it was to hard for benjmain to describe it. As he noticed the neck of the machine.

The machine ends with a neck with a cock pit on the end of it was fully computerised and it ahd systems Benjamin did not know yet that he was the one that created it although he ahd said it to himself before tat he thought it looked familiar. And he thought he had created it.

Every component every system everything about the machine and the colour the words that ran down it self be even more so the technology.
Benjamin was just about to blow his mind away right I to a different world as he noticed that the things in the machine fitted his mind perfectly.

And what was in front of him was created by him the scientists were there to remind him. Benjamin wanted in Lucy never caught on he had noticed that Benjamin knew what she had created had come form his mind.

Lucy after an hour or so of watching Benjamin finally invites him in to her office a conversations starts and like always turns=in to an argument
Benjamin was disagreeing Lucy was comp tempt on lying about his mind that machine came out from.

Lucy was still denying Benjamin and acting like he was a second class citizen and it did not exist what was created was done made and created by her and her science team it was just coincidence that he was in the place at the same time. Benjamin could not defied that fact that there was a science here. He could clearly see them.

Benjamin voice is getting louder he was speaking loudly but nice and calmly he was not shouting loud enough to cause any kind of disturbance to anybody mostly the scientists that were behind the extremely large high glass screens and long balcony's.

Benjamin was still good after an hour stating to lucy and still arguing that it has to be more than a coincidence a common coincidence everything seemed to fit in why was there and what he was there for and a few other questions.

Benjamin was getting close to her Lucy and Benjamin could see she was hiding some thing and she was slowly going to break Benjamin pauses realising what he was doing. He stops the conversation straight away apologises and leave the room, Lucy still up for it calls him back Benjamin took the pleasure of returning to her they continued to talk.

" Do you see that" Benjamins says quietly.
" see what" Lucy says hack to him.
" Do you hear that". Benjamín says again trying tio make a point he says it again softly.
" What is it Benjamin".
" wait".
Benjamin pauses as Lucy finishes his sentences that would send Benjamin back to his cell as he would be confident in finding out what he had created through his mind

Benjmain leaves the science laboratories and is heading back down stairs to his cell. By his choice as he passes through the security he shouts to Lucy who was putting the security back in to its position no body including benjmain could move.
Hay lucy I know your hiding something Benjamin calls out to her and I know it's a bout me benjmain says and I know it is about your stupid experiment.

As Benjamin speaks his words that come out of his mouth blows his mind away as he says the words that he says that he knows the experiment was about him and the machine.

Benjamin stops by his cell door Lucy was close by him in fact she was right by his side as she softly pushes Benjamin in to the room gently tells him to get in. this anger s Benjamin and another verbal fight begins. Os5 come down to the sell to sort things out.

Benjamin's guards were not the happiest as they chose not to speak they just acted on Lucy's behalf no communication just muscle all of them they were all the same in hight and there faces could not be seen they were hidden Lucy does not answer she tells him that hind some kind of helmet.
They were quite scary and could be aggressive Lucy had caught on.
Lucy hand Benjamin some tablets which he has to take she said it would am Benjamin down when he asks what they were there was no answer she tells him to take them Benjamin declines again making a good discission as he knew little about them. According to Lucy they would cleanse Benjamin's
mind and give him normal nice thoughts.

Benjamin was expected to take them or he would lose a full three months of the experiment straight away and they would all have to start form the beginning he would lose the knowledge in his memory it would take benjmain a little over a month to be re positioned in to the same position again.

Lucy tells Benjamin to have a think he has an hour. Benjamin was so impressed he throws them back at her. Lucy catches both of them. Lucy puts them back in to her pocket.

Benjamin calls out to her as she walks away back upstairs to her job Benjamin chases after her he calls out to her hay Lucy were benjmais words Lucy reply was a good one gone away you have waisted enough of my time. benjmain does not stop as he continues right up to the laboratory's doors he s stopped by the os5 guards.

As Benjamin tries tom get problem Lucy's stops she calls it a good move she tells the guard s to let Benjamin pass.

The three guards release Benjamin they look at each other as Benjamin makes an joke about what was under the mask he says it in a way like it ws a joke. The guards say nothing. Only to step aside.

Benjamin is free for the first time lucy and Benjamin were talking together with no shouting and no swearing benjmain and lucy were keeping this sweet.

Lucy knew that the time would come soon as it might as well be now, lucy had a lot of explaining to do. Benjamin was going to find out the truth about the whole experiment and the real reasons of why he had been held in the veracity for so long.

He says as he remembers and he is accepting the truth but with no memory of receiving any money which he needed.
Which was indecently was taken form him only to find that what he was experiencing now Benjamin was funding his own arrest and alibi and possible destruction.

He was paying for himself to has the experiments done it was a mind check and paying for the os5 grind syndicate it was as hard as doing time.

CHAPTER 7

Lucy agrees that Benjamin should be aloud back in the science labs to watch the team of scientist s to work. Benjamin was unimpressed with what he had found and the things that had come from inside of his mind first the machine and secondly everything else which conti9inued to flow through Benjamins mind, knowledge.

Benjamin is in happy to be upstairs again and there are smiles od=f welcomes coming form the whole team which give Lucy's plans for Benjamin away.
Benjamin starts to question why he ws there and benjmain asks Lucy in front of everybody for the truth.

Benjamin asks her again the reason for inviting him upstairs to the laboratory that evening.

Lucy shy's away for the first time slowly building up some bottle to answer Benjamin questions half the team would here them discussing something that ws private. This was typically Benjamin trying to get his own back on lucy for forcing him to be there and this seemed to be a routine as there arguments always seemed to be when Benjamin is in the laboratory's with Lucy they did to argue any where else.
This would happen before Lucy's and Benjamins conversation turns in to a fully blown argument it had happened again.

Benjamin does not understand the machine he was not really made that aware of what it could really do. He was also unaware that once in side of it again he was the victim and at that moment Benjamin did not ever recall or ahd ever been told that the machine was foe him.

After a few days of getting over the shock and getting
back down and Benjamin being told to avoid the
laboratory's and lucy with Benjamin watches the re
building of the machine from a short distance behind
some large glass screens.

Benjamin is realising that his future was really close he
was getting that strange feeling over his again you now
the scary feeling that you would get as you would get in
to some thing that you would think that was un safe.
Benjmain was thinking about doing it but dong it all
alone.
He was going to make a run for it however not out side
off the premises but into the machine Benjamin once
again was thinking hard knowing that the machine was
in complete takes the chance he knew that they could
not follow him yet he also knew that they would try.
And knowing that he designed the machine he would
have no problems finding the extra parts that he ahd
removed to make it fully work again.
However Benjamin catches on he is behind the large
tall heavy glass screens he would have to get what he
wants.

Lucy is busy watching everything that is done and everybody that is in motion everything that moves ion her laboratory. Lucy to ahs a few problems also which she wants resolved technical problems as she is talking to a robot and not Benjamin which would have been suited everybody including her team plus Benjamin

Lucy was to shy to call to Benjamin for some help mind you benjmain was close by her and when a guard leaks information that Lucy was losing it was a bonus of Benjamin to hear he comes to the conclusion that it ws not just him that was being screwed up. He would be looking at Lucy in a different way as she was losing her mind,

Benjamin kind of felt sorry for her however she was being and feeling cruel and said nothing for a few hours and left her self in a locked room with the do not disturb sign ion her door.

It was only going to be a matter of time before she cracks right on her own door step in front of everybody including her boss.

As Lucy looks upwards with the obvious expression ion her face with the look of doubt to go with her new look notices Benjamin he was talking to the robot which was talking back to him he found the robot fascination as Benjamin finishes his conversation and walks off before lucy could catch him.

Lucy rises slowly form her seat staring straight at Benjamin who in return gives lucy the finger and stares back from a distance lucy in return speaks in to her intercom which was placed by he ride on her belt it was small device like a pager just a little more futuristic.

Benjamin knew that Lucy was playing dirty and she did not want to talk to Benjamin let alone she him and in a bad mood calls for the security to collect him and take him back down stores to his room.

Benjamin already knew what lucy had done as Benjamin is being taken down stairs but not before some bad language and some shouting. With some

pushing and shoving from Lucy's guards the os5 grind
syndicate

Benjamin tells the guards the two of them to keep there
hands off him however the more he asked the more
that he was pushed if the back and nudged forwards
Benjamin fort back every time he ws shoved he tried to
shive them back. Benjamin was a little to short as his
head only reached the guards chest only. The more
attention he got which Benjamin thought it was funny
as everything he had said seemed to work in reverse.

Benjamin was in a mood for playing and once back in
his room he starts to draw up some plans the plans were
about the machine tor even why he chose to re draw
them he drawing were of the things that he thinks are

missing such as the components new ideas and things that should have been put in the machines systems.

Not knowing what he ws doing and not knowing what he ws going to do with them or who he ws going to sell them to why he had made them. However it seemed like a good idea at that time.

Benjamin is watching Lucy she is on the phone who she was calling Benjamin could not know as good as his hearing was Benjamin trying to listen hears nothing. However once the call was over and as according to Lucy s reaction and actions it was not a good conversation Lucy did not look to happy.

Benjamin knows tat his new plan the things that he missed on purpose would or could fix the machine he had the plans that the team of scientist needed.
After wards he was shouting in his cell ta it was him that created it through his mind Lucy did not know about Benjamin outburst and that evening Benjamins mind was answered.

Benjamin knows that he had been screwed over there was non pay check three months turned in to six and the contract was lost and with it Benjamin rights. He to now had that look of astonishment on his face like he had been really ill and screwed as his state of mind nothing else

As for that moment once again Benjamin as symptoms just set in the paranoia and all of the agonising hallucinations and then the paranoid thoughts it looked like lucy had got her own back.
and it looked like she was not the only one Benjamin too looked like he was suffering both the condition That had not gone unnoticed.

Lucy finally agrees that she could do with some help from benjmain as she leaves the labatory and goes off to find him he is closer to her than she had thought. Once lucy ahd found him and convinced him that he ws needed that again meant once again Lucy would have to get out her check book benjmain was not convinced and asks her why she approached him that way.

It was because Benjamin liked talking about money in fact if you through a coin on to the floor and lost it Benjamin could find it. He would be their with out no doubt to pick it up.

Benjamin and lucy discuss the deal however not before Benjamin slips up while trying to be clever
A making conversation about the new plan for the machine as he tells Lucy by mistake that he had drawn up the rest of the plans for the machine as he explains that the first set of plans were in complete.
Benjamin had already been seen handling them lucy did not want to disappoint Benjamin, but she already knew.
Lucy smiles and Lucy turns around and paces fast towards the large glass electronic doors in to a safer position.sk him for the new plans and drawings
Benjamin is a little reluctant to hand them over.

Lucy has her claws out getting ready to snatch them out of Benjamin's hand s which she did just she had them holding them tightly leaning back out of Benjamin's reach who incidentally was smiling

Benjamin stands there motionless thinking about what he had just done.

Lucy now has the rest of the plans and within a couple of months the machine will be re made and would be up and working. Benjamin was busy talking to himself and giving Lucy a good hard slagging off behind her back. As he speaks telling himself that he should have been more carful and thinking to himself that how could of he been so stupid and so naive

Benjamin was in his cell banging on the cell door lightly as if in a rhythm he is demanding that he wanted to speak with lucy.
Lucy on the other side was trying to avoid him as for what ahd happened earlier on in the morning wit the paper work. Lucy on the other hand was busy with the new information she was deciding weather or not she should i9nvite Benjamin upstairs to watch the finishing of his machine being made.

Benjmain was gripping his teeth as well as the cell door when he finds out that he had been invited up stairs his mind was ready to explode with anger and frustration and everything else that goes through the mind when being used.

Lucy finally gives in and within minutes Benjamin is back up stairs but not before expressing a few words about why he had called upon him and what was the plan.

Benjamin agrees that he would stick to Lucy's plans she makes him swear to it however Benjamin did not believe in all of that making promises and such things he was not in to making deals he thought the greeting and the opportunity was rubbish if he was there and if he was not there and he could not keep his mind tough that was Benjamin s deal no shaking of hands and know defiantly no signing of contacts there was no verbal agreement, not even as friends.

Benjamin gets to work the second thing he does is remove two of the engines as he speaks conducting the science team asking them what were they doing as Benjamin has to repeat himself.

As they answer Benjamin as they had other ideas Benjamin tells them to stick to his plan it would be safer, as he says those words some component explodes.

Benjamin's continued see what happens when you do not listen. Oh boy you find a replacement.

Benjamin being involved only caused more tension nobody could work and Benjamin was fully focused and ws giving everybody there orders he new so much he could of built the machines himself by himself. Lucy could feel the tension also.

No body was interested in Benjamins theory's of re educating them they needed to know benjmain or they were out.

Benjamin is busy taping in the coordinates in to the machines computer systems and checking for any problems and making sure everything I in order and working properly he is busy triple checking it everything as he knows needs to be perfect and clean also knowing now that it would be him in the seat traveling through his mind with the machine as guidance.

Benjamin for once seemed to be relaxed and feeling and looking normal for once it looked like lucy was feeling the same way he obviously had made a presents. They both were content and happy.
Benjamin wants to make a request and had time his question at the right time he asks lucy if they could shut the shutters as their was to much light, lucy anted to know why.
Benjamin continued that their was to much light coming in to the laboratory and it was effecting his vision.

Lucy thinking about what he had said agrees and has the shutters closed Benjamin can finally reach the part of the machine that he could not reach as t[for the lighting in the laboratory. Lucy wanted to ask Benjamin a question as if to imbarest Benjamin but it did not you will need theses a darker pair of glasses if you want to work everybody agreed so it was done.

Benjamin tries them on then takes them off telling Lucy that his eyes were fine and the glasses she gave him were to dark.

CHAPTER
8

As the machines had been re readied and re prepared
Lucy's frustrations and fascinations and the worry's of
Benjamin had come to stand still in away Lucy and
Benjamin had found the truth they were both making an
ameens and their relationship had re started it had
kicked in and every other day from that day looked
good and things were running smoothly once again.

Benjamin was looking more comfortable around her
and the science team. Lucy had dreamt that he would
notices her and by herself she thought that Benjamin
looked good.
Lucy too could finally relax, had Benjamin had
changed for the last few months benjmain was finally
finding his freedom it was all down to Lucy.

Benjamin work was nearly done he did not want to
leave the project the os5 grind syndicate were on there
way.

Benjamin was back in his cell he was trying to talk about what the experiences he had been having. It was not as if he had been through all the systems on the machine before.

While Lucy was playing being god again Benjamin was or felt like he was a gerbil in an extremely small cage Benjamin close his eyes as Benjamin is watching the images move he guesses that what he is experiences is part of the symptoms.

With all the watching Benjamin falls asleep only to wake up the very next evening he was out cold and had missed a whole morning it was lucy who woke him up Benjamin was obviously tired wake up Benjamin was her words she was hardly the loving type as she nudges Benjamin hard to get his attention. As she speaking to him telling benjmain that they were ready.

As Benjamin awakes and had not heard Lucy's conversation with him ahs to repeat everything she had said previously to him again. Benjamin rolls back over he wanted to sleep.

Benjamin I now a where that Lucy is there by his side and questions her why she ws in his cell and by her side was an another associate was leaning right over him as Benjamin pushes him away Lucy takes the pushing as a sign of aggression there experiment is put on hold for another day.

Even so now that Benjamin was awake and was enjoying the surprise of knowing that the machine was made and ready for him.

not quite he expected as they conversation started of with anger from both sides.

Benjamin was un impressed with his audiences Lucy was there to keep them away and him clam his audience was there also to make hm feel better.

He did not feel nothing and he kept his real feeling about the whole idea of doing the experiment live to himself the idea of just the experiment for him self ahd went out of the window. Lucy was in full control he wanted to be the first in to the machine which he was.

Benjamin also wanted in it looked like Lucy was aa good judge of character as Benjamin was willing to give up his life. They both knew that if something would go wrong they both would have to bare the consequences.

It was nearly time it was time for Lucy and Benjamin to discuss the facts of the journey that Benjamin was going to take. And the real reasons for his detainment in to the os5 grind syndicate. As they discussed the machine and how it should work all the parts were there it was working.

Lucy and benjmain have the chance to talk about things normally the real reasons of why they had built the machine to go with Benjamins mind which came form his mind. They were going back in time through his mind and also in to the future.

Benjamin was neither excited or impressed as lucy continued to talk and fill Benjamin in about the mission.

The last time they hunted the microchip it was left with some gang Lucy recalls however Benjamin reminds her that it felt close by.

Still never the less lucy was unimpressed also and continued and thought she had the same thoughts as Benjamin and they were both wasting there time as it was a job for Lucy and just some thing to play with for Benjamin.

The topic of the subject now was that it was neither in any body's hands the future was based on the microchip. It was common sense that they should go back to the very start back in time where it had been placed and found it was also common sense that they should also avoid places that they had been to.

The machine was ready one year and six months
everything was prepared and lucy was ready to go.
Benjamin was ready to buckle up. He ws in for the ride
of his life he was ready.

As Lucy buckles him in double checking not thinking
but thinking about the end result, Benjamin
Feeling cocky he is also filled with confidents.
Hay he says to lucy push the last brake in to position
good luck lucy says as she finishes fixing Benjamin in.

Will I need it Benjamin says
Lucy's reply ws one of confidents she reply's excited,
possible she says. Benjamin your on your own Lucy's
says that she was like a cobra in a angry mood
benjmain looks at her weirdly but knowing what she
ahd meant for said if her last words to Benjamin had
any meaning.

Benjamin believes in himself he was ready lucy looks
one last time at the scene ." he is ready". She says. All
the switches starts turning them self on and off
Benjamin is on his way.

Not forgetting what benjmain was actually looking for
the microchip Benjamin awakes with a thump
It was not the greatest of awakening that he had. At
least this time he woke up in one piece. Once Benjamin
was back in control of his life so he was content in
pressing the buttons on his specially made jacket
around the shoulder area. Speaking in to it and letting
the team back out side of him know tat he was on his
way. Benjmain was safe he had made it so far.

Lucy was feeling finished as for Benjamin who was
busy thinking it was a good feeling and making in and
through his journey in one piece proved that all the
calculating was perfect,
Everything that had happened to him was the opposite
of what the os5 rind syndicate wanted Benjamins street
party was hardly over his mind was in a some gang
bang in LA. The perfect place to start looking for the
microchip.

It was like he had never been their before he ws
confused and the microchip was not where Benjamin
thought it would be.

Benjamin his the dirt with disappointment as they ahd got it wrong it ws not Benjamins faulty and he had to go where the machine sent him. As benjmain picks himself up dusting himself off as he looks at the damage of the velocity of him hitting the ground Benjamin picks himself up off the concrete ground. Within less than a minutes he is good again.

Benjamin was looking around a lot more it seemed to be working although he was un aware of his new surrounding's and not sure where he was. Everything around him was real he was in the future but not in his future he was Lucy future he did to know this until latter on he return thinking who's mind is he playing with his or Lucy's future.

Benjamin once back and waisted was told to get some rest he would go back in tomorrow something seemed different and in him he could not rest the atmosphere was the only word he could explain the experience. Before Benjamin gets to eat and sleep lucy send him up stars for a medical benjmain refused until he was forced the side effects had already set in.

By now Lucy's team had taken over Benjamin was still shouting Lucy tells the os5 to get him up stairs and out of the eyes of his fans Benjamins business out side.

Benjamin is slowing down as he is dragged away with the last piece of his energy. It looked like Benjamin had done his job the machine was working everybody was happy and while Benjamin slept it off Lucy was busy upstairs partying and receiving the compliments she sorted after.

Benjamin could not believe it that Lucy had double crossed him Benjamin now had an extremely hard fight ahead of him not just his mind but his life let a lone.

Lucy has the machine and was returning her self back upstirs as for Benjamin he was trying to forget a few things the main thought was of the microchip they still had not found it and it controlled everything and every journey.

That the machine takes not only this but every mind that enters the machine while in the machine.

Lucy shouts just in time Benjamin was saved as a just before being thrown off an extremely high building.

"What oh its you", Benjamin was always ready to talk when these situations occur. Lucy was just greeting Benjamin. Only to receive a slap in the face only when she asks him again for the microchip. Benjamin is trying to sweeten her up only for lucy to hit him again with another slap around his face and then an apology.

"Would you mind stop doing that I get your point".
Benjamin s says to her. " Give me what I want".
Lucy had changed in a big way. " I know you have it so
give it to me give me the microchip and ill let you go".
Benjamin asks half joking if she ws up for a negotiation
lucy is getting rough verbally again she says give me
the microchip. Give it to her and they could cut a new
deal. Ill prove it Lucy calls her guard's off Benjamin.

Giving Benjamin time to step away from the edge of
the small wall with the large drop in front of him. As he
looks upwards watching the sky and casually opens a
packet of cigarettes.
Which was given to him by one of the guards some
time ago. Only to stumble a little forwards closer and
nearly over the edge. Only to feel his weakness he
lights up the cigarette and puts it in his mouth. Taking
another small step forwards and then again another step
forwards as he gets closer to the edge of the building.
Benjamin takes a large breath as his mind watches the
change in the sky's as the clouds changes with the
weather.

Lucy watching closely raises her b[voice it was heading in to Benjamins direction which was correct and made sense she ws still shouting give her the microchip Benjamin had not fund itv yet and lucy was going on like she was hysterical or something. She continued that they could make a deal.

Meantime at that same time lucy was banging on about some deal that they could make with said nothing at the end of her words she knows where Benjamin is he is out side up on stop of one of there roof tops. Both of them thinking why was he there as he was supposed to be in his future by the machines maybe lucy thought that ws his future for now.

Benjamin does not understand it either Lucy has to explain. And hopes that Benjamin does not jump. Lucy and Benjamin could see eye to eye and it looked like they had both come to an agreement they were making. They both felt by themselves that they were both acting greedy Benjamin for the money of course and obviously Lucy for the microchip.

Benjamin takes a few steps backwards from the edge of the building s ledge. The only thing that was keeping Benjamin upright was the wind blowing in front of him nudging him backwards as it blew in his direction.

Lucy really gives her self away it was clear to herself
that she was lying and she nearly mentions the word her
thoughts of hoping that Benjamin would jump.
Benjamín steps further away from the edge of the
building s he was now sitting down uncured

Lucy tells Benjamin to come in to her room her office
they could talk inside and make a deal Benjamin
seemed to be thinking differently he was transfixed in
some thing else his mind was else where. Lucy was
looking at him and Benjamin was looking at her
strongly like he had lost something like his mind.

Benjamin was looking at her like she was a completely
and totally stranger it was like they had never met.
Benjamin and lucy were discussing what had just
happened they both agreed that they both where acting
a little out of character.

Benjamin apologises handing the microchip over to
Lucy her eyes widen it looked under the microscope
veery rich in afct extremely rich as she picks up the

small object smaller than a pin head this microscopic piece of technology that ws also needed to run the machine in the correct manor.

Benjamin had felt like he had been cheated mind you its was better of being at the top of the building waiting to be thrown off.

Benjamin closes his eyes he is on his bed down stairs wishing that he had not been thought about as it was his problem it was his attitude that was letting him down it was his attuite that forced him to fail on that's occasion. However it was not at a loss lucy gives Benjamin second chance a chance to re prove himself Lucy's offers him a job. He was tested lucy says he could go in and he could come out. Benjamin gets the respect that he wanted in his relationship.

Benjamin was called back up stairs not straight away but after a few days after there relationship had settled. Benjamin was boasting and was neatly suited up in some kind of suit that the science team had created for him. He was now looking the part.

Benjamin wanted to know what te suit ws for lucy tells him that it would keep him safer when in the machine. It works Lucy continued with her head down finishing her notes that they ahd just finished making it and he was going to test it for them and himself. She continued that it was part of the experiment now.

Benjamin looks at her in a really strange way. They have time she said however things cam change quickly so be warned go on Benjamin get in to the machine. That ws more like a warning to get in to the machine thana welcoming Benjamin thought.

Even so Benjamin takes his chance and get s in to the cock pit. Benjamin is excited and calls to Lucy does the machine have a name yet. Once again Benjamins ego leaves Lucy unimpressed.
Benjamin gets no answers and he knew why everything was coming back to his mind. Benjamin was totally frilled with what he had created a machine that could travel through your own mind with everything connected Benjamin was back in business again.

Benjamin was called back in to the laboratory he ws feeling a little better only for the fact that lucy was there that he complained. The morning was nearly over and benjmain was just about to stud=ff his face Benjamin caused a stand still he ws in the wrong frame of mind. As he approaches the science team.

Benjamin was abstract he was else where he was focusing on the way that Lucy was treating everybody and her self Lucy was acting in the totally opposite way that you would think she was.
Unsure and in sane Benjamin ahd called it. As for backing her up and the opposite the experiment looked like it had taken over her not just mentally but physically. Lucy for the first time was making bad discissions.

Lucy did not know but Benjamin was still in his mind waiting and waiting for the compliments Benjamin was now asleep but he was also awake and once feeling surprised he walked lucy ws using him to star the experiment. Benjamin claimed to her that he needed more time his eyes closed like he ws watching some thing. As he brushes his teeth with lucy waiting for an answer behind him.

His face blunt like he had been using some thing recreational which was a lie it was the in and out of what was actually going on that Benjamin was being warned about.

With the next few days Benjamin was knacked his face showed all of the system's that the scientist said that he would show he sound s few more days in the doctors room recovering. His face had changed and his life ws different. His energy was gone and he ws feeling ten times more older and tired than he actually was.

Benjamin is standing alone wishing that he never crated the machine. Like with any super hero there comes a price a curse perhaps its has its us and its downs and its consequences Benjamin was trying to understand what he had been created
Deep down in his heart he wanted to destroy it however he made for a good purpose it was made to stop the destruction of the earth. The total destruction of the planet earth.
Lucy and Benjamin ahd already discussed this topic they both agreed to stop talking about the subject while around their science team.
That conversation would exist again not now but well in to the future.

Benjamin was chilled out all the stress of everything that they had been talking about and the short trip with the machines was done it was Lucy's turn for the next move. Lucy was still acting like she was at the top and on top of things in the laboratory and her situation of leading the experiment.

However through Benjamin's eyes her method was a total mess and she needed somebody to tell her it was hard enough as it was as it was going to come from Benjamin.

Benjamin was pacing around in his cell trying to fin th e right words to tell her with out upsetting her. As he paces up and then down as he counts his steps in trepidation as he practising his lines there a knock at his door Benjamins stops and he waits Benjamin is well prepared as he walks to his door looking down wards at his shoes. Stretching one arm out and reaches for the door handle ass he looks through the small glass window the viewing glass.

Only to be greeted by Lucy. " What do you what"
Benjamin calls out moving back wards giving him
some more space as the os5 guards s were there.
Lucy speaks." I do have a key Benjamin so keep it
polite and open the door.
Look Benjamin the machine is ready again for you so
come on".
Lucy could of put it together a little more normal as
she sounded like he was in a nursery like she was
talking to child.
Lucy catches on and refreezes it "look Benjamins".
She has raising her voice "would you get your ass
upstairs when you are ready the team are waiting for
you".

Benjamin has no time to think even so it was his call
and he was in his cell door that had been opened he ws
now face to face with the os5 grind syndicate as he
takes his step out side of his cell the guards hands him
his pass card. Benjamin was granted and he could walk
in and out and down corridors as much as he liked he
was free but only for a short time.

Benjamin was late he knew it was to good to be true the whole thing stunk the nostalgia of the whole process was making benjmain feel dizzy he had become extremely light headed and disorientated and he needed to sit down.

" What's going on ". He asks.

Knowing exactly where he sat which was in the machine again Benjamin, s asks what is going on. And on his second attempt the machine speaks and gives Benjamin the answer that he was looking for.

Lucy did not know about this neither did the science team. Everybody in the room was silent for a few minutes " it can speak."

" How"

The compliments kept on rolling in. Benjamin was now feeling the same way as Lucy who too still could not understand what Benjamin had created.

Lucy was right in front of Benjamín asking him to explain Benjamin knew position she continued where going to give you a little some thing to keep you nice and calm.

" keep me calm I could not feel any cooler".

" it will keep you nice and cool as you put it through the journey".

" journey" Benjamin says ".

" Yes" Lucy says

What ever Lucy had given benjmain it seemed to be working he was high however feeling the same. But it seemed like he was in more control of his mind some how.

Benjamin was off to find the microchip an the os5.
Lucy was gong to have a lot of explaining to do when
Benjamin gets back home.

CHAPTER 9

Benjamin was having fun all day he ws in the lab s
kitchen things were hoting up as Benjamin is at the
stove cooking while he is stuffing his face with lots of
trades such as ice cream and anything lese he could find
to eat. The chef was around Benjamin entertaining him
until Benjamin gets board only then to ask the chef to
cook him meal. The chef was delighted benjmain
wanted chicken while knocking back the last fifth of the
can of beer which he had found on the side.

As the chef is busy telling himself that Benjamin
actions were of good nature and they were fine.
It was weird Benjamin thought as he was meeting one
of his neighbours. It was very rarely that Benjamins
would he welcomed in to the kitchen. Only benjmain
could see his total vision was again totally the opposite
of what he expected of a normal reaction from a normal
experience.

Benjamin puts his hand out greeting all od f them as he marches in to the space made for him in the kitchen. This was all made up in Benjamin s imagination which was the problem and the reason why os5 grind syndicate wanted him out of the way.

However Lucy saw things a little different and was fully on Benjamin's side Benjamin had lost all feeling s for Lucy and has his last greeting with a man that looked at them all of the science they looked the same still. Benjamin knew that it was his imagination it could never be less.

Benjamin was snow by his window his TV ws loud and the sound was up. Nobody near him could hear his thoughts.

Benjamin was slightly out of his mind and out of his face his fitness was his buzz. It was his fix. It was not to the fact

However things were about to change he was going to stand up in a new habitat two of them Benjamin knew o this and was swell prepared. It was not like him to start was no fact that he was going to hide parts of his personality it was a plus on his own behalf as he enjoyed that kind of thing this was going to happen soon.

Benjamin wanted to move quickly he wanted to get back in to the machine he felt that he was over ready never worked he just wanted to get in to the cock pit.

Benjamin was on and he kept on complaining Lucy could see the frustration on his face Lucy thinks Benjamin is trying ng to waist time he was not even so Lucy hurrys things along while breaking a few of her own rules believing tat benjmain would be in a better position. Once again as Lucy makes things work for her benjmain and lucy once again starts a conversation that turns in to a verbal disagreement and a conversation that becomes an argument

Lucy was telling Benjamin straight that the machine runs with him in it or it does not run at all with the experts by his side she says not him she continues to argue with benjmain bring him down a peg or two then a little bit more just to her self good and to feel a little better about her situation.

Benjamin had put and was putting pressure on everybody with his attitude and complaints even the small people in the building especially in the laboratory the kitchen staff were getting a totally different message benjmain had changed.

Benjamin was feeling freed and he was waiting changing his personality he had gone form being the nice person to being a monster a rude and aggressive person he had become horrible Lucy wanted the old Benjamin back they all did they wanted to make a personal professional move on Benjamin just to bring him done a step or two.

Lucy says it was for his own good.

Benjamin had over stepped his mind again lucy was their to bring him down. Benjamin was having fun he had tuned in and was listening to an conversation about himself by lucy. Lucy was talking about their previous arguments there arguments seemed to turn toward some she said. Benjamin listens closer this time he walks in to her office nice and rude while shouting at Lucy while walking in to her conversation.

Lucy was just running out of words and Benjamin was shouting at her losing control finding himself in Lucy last position as she takes control -only to realise they were going to be in her office all day long. The scientists were looking in as another conversation which started quietly became as loud as an erupting volcano as leaving her office watching the window s vibrate ready to fall apart.

Benjamins face drops with the feeling of guiltiness and returns the comments that could of needed the conversation. Lucy switches off and the argument comes to its end. Benjamin leaves via the opening of the office door as he slams the door behind him letting his presents known.

Before he gets the chance to catch it shuts quickly as he turns his attention to his staff and while shouting at them Lucy walk's back in the scene walking past Benjamin and in to her office and takes a seat in her office chair.

CHAPTER
10

Benjamin was well on his way to hell regard s to Lucy experiment Lucy was discerned about Benjamin future all she wanted to do is achieve the experiment. The only thing that really seemed to be right was that they were both sane. While writing down lies through the experiment thinking that it actually meant something to Lucy but in fact it did not mean a thing and if lucy thinks that she was gowning to end up in some kind of magazine she was wrong.

Os5 owned the project, and they would met again in the near future. Benjamin was less impressed and wanted to know what lucy was thinking and if she could send in one of the other bad guys in first.

Benjamin already knew so there ws no point in arguing Benjamin was feeling as little low for the first time however he was well prepared. He was a strong person not just in his mind but in his body also.

Benjamin and Lucy were both excited about the machine it was newly prepared and benjmain ahs two days of rest. Lucy on the po0ther hand needed to speak to Benjamin once again the ins and out of the experiment and the plans of the machine they needed a lesson and a fast one again.

He would be traveling first through his mind aided by the machine its was an extremely sensitive and a gamble only in the machine however lucy had to test it she seemed to believe that the future of science was science.

Benjamin gets in to the machine cot pit and makes himself comfortable. As Benjamin questions himself anion what he was doing and that a he must be crazy. As he buckles up further in to the cot pit Benjamin was at last acting like he was in the right frame of mind.

He was serious and he got his attitude spot on. Lucy ws looking baffled and Benjamin seemed to look like he knew what he was doing.

Everything was in order that day was the day that Lucy was praised for the project as it was the first day of the actual experiment.

Benjamin had gone through the machine and way back in to his mind.

He knew doing what he was doing was a surprise and looking for this microchip which if he could find it they could save the world.

Benjamin awakes not recognizing his surrounding so he knows that he had got inside of his mind he thinks that he is in the cells in the unit only to fin himself back in his apartment.

Benjamin is quick to takes off his suit and some clothes he was moving quickly never the less even though he had just arrived in company by his door. Benjamin was not on his own he gets a call through his mind that a computer visual will be arriving very soon it did it was Lucy a hologram. Benjamin again questions his team he says tat he thought he was working alone Benjamins reply was a what and then he gets an answer that it was a surprise regards to the hologram. Benjamin says he is flattered

Benjamin tips just in time to welcome lucy as she puts a few things in place mostly her presents some thig that Benjamin would have to do and get used too.
She was there to back up Benjamins plans. She was in the machine, Benjamin asks for some guidance as for what was happening out side of his apartment. Lucy presents and her own systems finally kick in benjmain already has the idea to that bad company was on its way. Lucy was cool she was by his side.

Lucy is still just a hologram was by his side nobody could seen but Benjamin apart form Benjamin and things were made easier. They both agreed. Benjamin is controlled to a cabinet down stairs.

In his apartment there was an invitation to a cellar where they would find a lot of fire power. Which Benjamin would later on use. As he has company.

Benjamin knows that he has got trouble coming and just as he thought about what was coming it arrived. Benjamin gets a fright for the first time he goes cold turkey. Benjamin was actually afraid for once. This was not good timing Benjamin was in trouble and it took him about a minute exactly to find himself only for that one minute to end so that he could pull himself back together. As he continued to unlock and load his arsenal of weapons.

Benjamin closes his eyes watching that he was someplace else however this was not going to happen he feels like he is being watched however there was nobody there.

Benjamin cocks his weaponed the second within that minute, making them bot ready to use. As he puts them both down. Benjamin walks to his window looking at them on the table. There was an early morning sun set and a tranquil blue sky with the white heavenly clouds.

It could not have been more perfect timing for Benjamin, he was laughing slowly realising that everything already had been put in to place. Benjamin's mission was done.

As Benjamin is close to his first target in the future this ws his concern the mind damage as he might come back as a vegetable. A different persona disabled his other concern as he is told the target could be at the very end of his mind at the very end of his past.

However Lucy was there to guide him correctly. making sure that there are no mistake. Lucy did not get things wrong. Benjamin unimpressed says to Lucy in the wrong way on purpose. Lucy understands staying calm sends them both back into the past. This time they find nothing however there was clue about where the microchip could be the second micro chip in fact the first one was also already in their hands.

Benjamin was in shock when Lucy had told him that there ws a second microchip. Lucy laughs telling Benjamin what did he think all the work all of the fighting what do you think we were about.

Benjamin knew this and corrects his position one down benjmain says refereeing to the microchip as he says one to go come on lucy who's next. Benjmain asks Lucy was unimpressed she did not like Benjamin new attitude when it came to the killing.

Look she says to him I don not mind the fact that I am part of your job but you can keep the thought of killing your targets to your self they are listening up there lucy points upwards and whisper they can hear us.
Benjamin understood but he did not care. Lucy finishes the conversation quietly. Benjamin looks at her asking her quietly if she was serious.

I am removing the biggest load of scum you should be happy up stair's. Lucy butts in Benjamin steps aside pulling Lucy over with him for a word of encouragement. As he continued that it was his life which was on the line and not hers and it ws him that could become a vegetable if he steps in the wrong place walk's the in the wrong way or even smiles worth out there permission so do not start all that fancy be polite bull crap that you seem to think that would do me some good.

Lucy says nothing Benjamin continued that's was better lucy on the other hand did nit catch on and continued if you really did not lie the mission we can go back and start it all again.
Benjamin took that last comment as a joke. Benjmain within that last conversation finds a better way of removing his targets it did motivate him that long to find another answer.

It was not long Benjamin finds the answer although he was way back in the past he has an idea he had to make sure that it worked.

Benjamin is complaining and arguing with Lucy that if she could not handle all of the blood shed she should of chose a different another partner.

Lucy was sacked with Benjamins final answer as Benjamin comes to end of their conversation Lucy wasted to speak however nothing, nothing came and no words come to her mind.

That long silence was a first for Lucy as she would normally have some thing to say. As Lucy turns way Benjamin is reading her mind. And butt sin to the conversation leaving a message in courage meet to answer her last sentence as she did this time it was to Benjamin.

A message in side as lucy and Benjamin lower there weapons Lucy starts another conversation all about Benjamin who in return gathers up all the notes on Lucy that he could think about. Lucy ws closer to his mind.

Benjamín was in trouble Lucy approaches Benjamin
who has no council

There arguments re starts Benjamin is in and is within
doubt as Benjamin has to protect him again with his
science team.
Benjamin mind was else where as he waited in darkness
with lucy waiting for their next orders and a possible
ride in the machine.

Benjamin getting in to the machine he as to relax and feel no pressure just nice and relaxed Lucy's words were are you chilled. She was and she was acting cool. Lucy ask s him again are you cool as she leans over to him. Benjamin agrees that he was fine as he shouts s to her then is told not to shout.

Benjamin looked puzzled and is complaining to himself. Benjamin is in a place where everybody can hear him even hear him breathing if they wanted too. Lucy smiles as the sound of her team becomes a silent one, lucy thinks about what ws in front of them and before her.

Benjamin takes his time as Lucy and himself takes control of the electronic cot pit Benjamin was about to make science history with lucy by his side.

It looked like from a short distance that the good guys Lucy and Benjamin were going to win they were on there away to receive their special microchip and kick some street ass while retrieving it.

Benjamin is ready he is buckled in the sound of his buckle echoed around the science laboroty as he quickly puts it in place as his mind kicks in to wat he was dong not once or twice but four times.

Benjamin was in two frames of mind as he sits waiting for his orders in the cot pit of the machine.

CHAPTER 11

As Benjamin is buckled in with security watching near by tapping a few switches while tapping their coordinates the ones which Lucy had given him the same as the science team were using as they had to be the same. Through the mind of course Benjamin was given the signal to jump in to his mind.

Point 1 point 2 point 3 point 4 point 5 I am in. Bingo Benjamin shouts then disappears, his body once referred by the machine was cold normal Lucy says. Benjmain once back again is taken to the sick bay.

Lucy ask the science team when would or how long his recovery would be they calculated no more than forty eight hours two days lucy smiles with agreement. As benjmain is wheeled out lucy stands looking impressed for once. The well done and congratulations party that lucy ahd to go to which gave her the chance to be her self and have a good boast about what she believes her experiments would achieve.

Benjmain had been left out as she was busy partying with her team as the rest of the results of the experiment.

Benjamin knew no different as he was resting he had fallen I to a deep sleep not knowing anything else. Lucy the next morning ahs to explain regards to Benjamin, once gain Lucy gives her team an explanation of why he was left out.

Lucy had left her self looking like a user these thoughts could be heard by Benjamin they were passing right through him some thing had changed. Benjamin mind ws open for thought.
It felt different it felt sane why should he not have those feelings those thoughts were now new and in place.

Benjamin continues and Lucy was no different yet. Benjamin knew non different and saw no different, it was a new feeling in Benjamins mind. Benjamin was going to a little problem putting his last thoughts to Lucy a round her mind and in her head.

CHAPTER

12

Benjamin needed to rest his mind and body are both tired and he ws feeling the kick of the whole episode in his mind as she stumbles across the laboratory floor in the experiment room.

It was true Lucy understood and realising that Benjamin ws telling her the truth he ws actually tired Benjamin walks in to her office chairs a clumsily move finally leaning up against her window watching the view like he ahd something to say.

Benjamin oases out cold the whole experiment was now
in jeopardy it looked like it had finally takes it's toll.
Lucy thought she could do it her self she was a little
reluctant to try and follow Benjamin as everything he
does by himself looks like a mistake.
It was just a run of bad luck lucy says she too ahd
changed her mind and had crashed out.

Benjamín and Lucy were both a sleep for the very first
time
Lucy for totally conked out through the next day and
the day after benjmain ws just out cold

Believing that he would have a better day tomorrow.

The very nest morning they wake simultaneously as he
awakes so does Lucy both bumping in to each other
while both looking for the bathroom nothing was said
as they stood side by side like a married couple which

they were not. While they both brushed there teeth and washed their faces.

Benjamín was the first to finish and leave Lucy was close behind him following him aa a few minutes later. Benjamin was now busy in his wardrobe. Lucy was now sure to be on her way,

Acting with no particular as she tries to chose and see the clothes that Benjamin was going to choose some thing near, close but nothing suggested that anything had be adjusted.

Benjamín was in a normal started of mind it was the usual experience as he floats through his mind as she looks while moving, looking at places and mostly at peoples doors anything that would bring them closer to the second microchip.

The microchip that could and would give Lucy the information that they were looking for. That information would be the information that would control the future of the planet earth. It had been hidden in Benjamin's mind and lucy and benjmain where in his mind looking for it and looking for the answers to find it.

Benjamin s symptoms had worsened his body was refusing everything he was going through some serious spiritual things. Benjamin mind was in a state as he battles to keep himself sane. Benjamin looks up wards he is denied as he has the feeling of nothing and Lucy could see this lucy had enough she wanted to call the experiment off.

Benjamin has the same idea but is not thinking. Lucy presses the button Benjamin shouts to her no Lucy had pressed the abort button. Benjamin was nearby there it ws only going to be a couple of seconds. Before Benjamin ahd reached his mind as Lucy waits it was only a few seconds before Benjamin starts to tell that he ws inside.

The os5 grind syndicate once again Benjamin was standing out side the large tower block
Waiting, watching, and observing what was the future.

Benjamin has to wait for Lucy her hologram as on its way to him. Benjamins timing was perfect this time they both were prepared.

As for the last time that Benjamin ended up in shock regard to lucy's appearance everything else ws running smoothly benjmain ws on top of the mind games especially his own. And he was expecting her soon. Lucy and Benjamin were now together both of them standing out side of the tower block.

It was gritty and not nice Benjamin could feel the surrounding s and it odd not have a very good welcoming feeling to the place. He questions Lucy asking her if they were in the right place. Lucy had agreed that there was some thing funny ton there place. They both agreed that it had the smell to it with every else it felt dangerous they both could feel this. Benjamin was walking in to something that he wished he had walked around.

Benjamin was looking for something a clue an answer he turns to Lucy she did not answer him because she did not know the answers to the questions. Either way it looked like they both were having to enter the large building. It was the machines fault it had brought them there so it had to be the right place. They both agreed.

The building was a dark one derelict and used however people still lived in it. It looked like it ws ready to fall down when Benjamin mentioned it lucy agreed. the tall, windows built in to every apartment and its cold doorways and its lengthy corridors looking forwards at each other with its concreted floor leading up to every door.

This is totally what Benjamin did not want in fact it ws the opposite however it was the same as Benjamin thought it would be he could walk straight in to it he was not in his future as the future that he was looking at was in the past

It looked like form the position that they were both in that Benjamin was suffering a little from surprised walking in to something unexpected. He would take a note of that as for reminding himself to look at the destination before they set off. Benjamin feels that he is un prepared poorly prepared for the mission that he ws on. Never the less Lucy was there backing him up.

As for Benjamin he could not move as for the situation that he was in as he was allergic to his own past. Even so once again Lucy as there to guide him, even her presents was enough to convinced him that he was safe. Benjamin looking at the hologram still not connived that it was a good idea when was he convinced lucy needed to find answer to Benjamin's problem's Benjmain was scared.

Benjamin was looking over his shoulder and out of the corner of his eyes not knowing what he was suppose to be expecting content in believing

That the was going to have his hologram by his side they both continued to work together.

Benjamin and lucy knew what they were looking for
was someplace home the tower block they were looking
for the microchip and Benjamin really believed that it
ws right in front of them some place in the tower tht
stood in front of them.

All Benjamin had to do is convince Lucy who was right
by his side that he was right lucy still having opposite
thoughts confirmed to flow Benjamin theory's.

Not because she did not believe in wht benjmain as saying because they were partner and that is a what a partner ws for. Within a few moments of Lucy speaking of this Benjamin gets upset and an another arguments starts lucy ws trying tom rephrase what she had meant as she correct her words her sentences as she knows that she had slipped up.

Benjamin agrees as Lucy re joined him after he switched her off the conversation starts again this time Lucy gets it right Benjamins behaviour towards her however it was not like Lucy not be able to talk about what she knows already. Lucy an Benjamin end that conversation leaving them both in silence with nothing else to discuss, talk about when it was like being back on dry land.

Lucy was smiling at Benjamin Lucy was drawn to the microchip Benjamin knew no difference Lucy was pushing him to make a move quickly she did not like the area that he was in. Benjamin has no choice but to approach the building Lucy requests it.

Now Benjamin was unsure of which area he was going to approach the tall building the tower block once in front of the block Benjamin taps in the coordinates they match telling benjmain that there was something up there waiting for them. There on the first floor with out any luck.

Only to move further only for the same to happen again Benjamin gets a reading but et nothing still they continue. Benjamin on his own for a while is getting frustrated.

He is looking down on the floor there's nothing there for him he can feel it he knows its in the building.

Benjamin looks down on the floor this time he s a couple of flights higher than he was near the top of the building in fact as notices a rock and ws just about to turn and walk away he gets the thought of picking up the rock and looking underneath of it.

To Benjamin surprise there is a set of keys except when he tries them in the door they do not fit. Even though

the keys have a key ring they do not have a number.
Benjamin continues climbing further up in the block.
Benjamin as avoiding the lifts he did not like them let a
lone trust them. He was to scared of a person he would
take the stairs.

Lucy was behind Benjamin complaining about how
many flights of stairs that she ws having to climb
Up. Making jokes on their way as lucy was only there
by Benjamin side as a hologram.
Benjamin could hardly laugh that one off as he is
actually struggling as to get half way Benjamin starts to
complain to himself.
Lucy was now busy pretending to feel sorry for
Benjamin predicament and defiantly about the position
that he ws in. Benjamin tarts a converstion while
partying as he reaches the fi]forty fifth level out of a
hundred floors.

Benjamin can feel the strain as he nears another floor
asking Lucy who was behind him if they were there yet.
Lucy answer no. come on Benjamin says it had to be
the top Benjamin is climbing up to the next floor
benjmain asks her again how they were doing lucy does
not answer.

He ws nt at the top but ws close to it, Benjamin was coming up to the next floor he could read the signs that were there to guide him he looks hard at the signs it said a level on it fifty one benjmain qs a bout to quite he thought that he ws at the top again.

Ok he says panting just a few more to go, benjmain and lucy were looking at each other
Benjmain ahs a question to asks her. If the microchip was really at the top of the block the very top of this building.

Benjamin was feeling a little disappointed he s looking at lucy she say yes its is really in there if that what your going to ask me. It was the microchip was in the last flat the top of the tower block in the building.

Benjamin as they both come up to the next floor which was a cold one fifty two Benjamin Lucy the same question again only to receive the same answer. Which ws correct which was the same as her first answer for him before Benjamin ahd found an answers to his question   it had already been answered.

As Lucy reaches the next flight of stairs telling
Benjamin it was clear and safe they both notice from
that level a large noise is coming form the area above.

How far above them they did know and Lucy was just
finding out for him. It looked like the microchip was
caught up in side of somebody's party right at the very
top of the tower Benjamin and lucy are closer to it Lucy
could feel its was pulling he towards it as for Benjamin
he felt nothing but Lucy's guidance.

Benjamin has to walk in to a party he was not
particularly happy about it Lucy knew and Benjamin
and Benjamin was losing control of his feeling s about
this his situation he lets Lucy know.

Benjamin is closing his eyes as they come to the one hundredth level of the blocks stairs. Benjamin finally compliments himself as for lucy who was behind him he says nothing to her.

As for the climb it was therapeutic counting the steps upwards forgetting tat he would have to count them back down. only to realised that the exercise was not over just yet.

Benjamin turns around to Lucy saying to her that he feels nothing just thinking about the descend back down wards to the very first floor.

Lucy thinks that she has made an mistake there was something not right there ws something missing what had Benjamin over looked lucy believed it was the microchip it was telling them warning them that they were too close to it.

Benjamin had enough he wanted out he did not believe and at that point Lucy's well made machine was being to conk out on Benjamin.
It looked like Benjamin was running out of time as he was heading back out of his mind to the os5 grind syndicate laboratory's

It looked like Benjamin had failed he could not find the os5 grind syndicate and the microchip it did not seem to matter a how many trips through the mind it would take.

Benjamin was looking hard at lucy they both wated the smile they both were disappointed and they both wanted another attempt.
Lucy was sure tht the microchip was there some where in that building Benjamin had reason ton believe the same he felt tat feeling as so lucy did. There ws no reason to complain as they both thought and felt the same.

Lucy wanted Benjamin to take another look there's a pause in her converstion until Benjamin agrees there was a feeling tat this n]may of happen and about the position that they were in including tee machine. However te team back at the os5 the verciiaty were losing there confidents.

Lucy and Benjamin give a quiet speech her words continued as they seemed to echo through the wall s of the building was not Benjamin the only person to notice. The lights have dimmed as Benjamin gets a little cocky after giving his speech walks away and gets in to the machine.

Lucy was all smiles as she is looking around for Benjamin her vison focused across the room lightening her own vision and Benjamin back ground lights up.

Lucy brings Benjamin all the way back all the way to the beginning of Benjamins mind. In a sense I suppose you could call it phycology as a phycological experience using a machine controlling himself back and forth through his mind. the meaning of science was about to change they could touch feel see anything through this attention it ahd actually started to work.

Lucy could not believe it Benjamin was again in two frames of mind. Once gain arguing over the fact of the fact that it as his doing and it was his mind and he wanted a few things for himself after the experiment.

Benjamin did not know that he was the only person with the right mind to fit in to the machine and lucy her self. With out Benjamin the project would be called off. lucy does not tell Benjamin about this information.

Benjamin was thinking dollars, money, pounds, with Lucy having to keep her word she has no choice but to agree.

Benjamin thinks he is well with in his rights to be asking the team for more money he was busy counting the months that he had been in containment.

Simply Lucy's experiment Lucy looks at him awkwardly as she is slowly agreeing to give Benjamin nothing. Then changing her mind s to say to him name his price then changing her mind as they play Benjamin say he names his price Lucy says that's not enough Benjamins eyes widen he give her some other number s Lucy's replies to high Benjamin smiles ok he says intrepadation and excitement one more bingo he it nailed it right.
 That's better Benjamin Lucy said
Benjamin thought he was going to walk out nothing and he knew what Lucy's was doing. Benjamin was watching her and was watching her closely as he would

get the chance again. Getting in to the machine once again occurred from his pervious journey.

Lucy looked and seemed like she was doing good with no problems this thought of Lucy getting in control made Benjamin think.

Benjamin was some to release that traveling through the machine only seemed to effect him nobody else had any symptoms for the simple fact that he was the only one who had used the machine and a few other scientist's before himself Benjamin said to himself that nobody else dared to try it.

Benjamin was in the canteen he is sitting down at the table playing with his food. Thinking and thinking again that there was somebody near him and that he ws not o his own. Benjamin looks at his watch four hours later until the re entry was going to be Benjamin was unaware of the time and unaware of what he was actually going to do to recall the whole plan again.

Benjamin sits reciting the whole plan idea through his mind not realising that his tapping om his table was getting louder. Until he misses it and taps on his plate.

Benjamin was concentrating he was thinking hard he ahd his own plans of how he should attempt to recover the microchip it was totally different to Lucy's.

Mind you Benjamin thought two heads where better than one and if he could not fulfil Lucy's plans he could have to full fil his own to back himself.
Benjamin hopes that he has made the right discission and his plans would work even though he stops tapping his fork on the table and puts back o his plate. Even though he thinks he has an answer his attuite does not change.

Benjamin was acting like he was going into space or something Benjamin looks deep in to the darkness of his surroundings. Benjamin is sitting quietly he is figuring things out the act at the canteen table as Lucy walks in to the room with smiles and joy of laughter speaking of the experiment however this did not last for to long

Benjamins looking for a verbal disagreement and lucy walked right in to it. After Benjamin had said his piece and Lucy being quick only lost by a word leaves Benjamin alone and leave s his space his surrounding's.

Lucy was startled as for what reason Benjamin would just kick off she ws baffled as she thought they both were on a level it looked like she had or seen some thing medical about Benjamin.

She does not recall starting the argument she finally catches on Benjamin was clearly upset and under the weather it was clear he was feeling aggressive

Lucy after a long conversation which was another long argument but on a level lucy did not speak and benjmain was doing all for the talking Lucy has to report Benjamin to the medical team Benjamin was not being Benjamin he ws back in his cell again.

Benjamin was in a strange mood as he calls to lucy form his cell believing that his words would reach through the large glass screens above him a dark place was in his mind which ws actually was. Benjamin asks if he could have some light that sentence ws enough for Lucy to lose her temper and shout and she continued for a number of minutes.

It all you Benjamin she ws shouting why can you not just except the space. He was not in the position to except or respect anything. And certainly if they were none of his concern and with that lucy asks Benjamin to sit down.

Benjamin was confronted not knowing what she ws talking about Benjamin was already in a mood and was a feeling cocky and lucy already knew that there ws something up with him. Before Benjamin gets a chance to speak Lucy raises her voice telling Benjamin to sit down.

Benjamin does as he is asked except the chair that Lucy was offering him was not there, they both look at each other. Lucy sits down at her desk on her chair Benjamin is left standing up. Benjamín was being confronted not sure about what lucy wanted to talk about.

As Lucy continued Benjamin finds himself sitting on her office floor he polity asks her if he was supposed to be on her floor with that Lucy smiles which ws un seen as they were both now in the dark.

Benjamin is seated in the office on the floor Lucy's reply to him and gives Benjamin apology as for having nothing for him to sit upon. Benjamin looks at her Lucy was just about to catch on as Benjamin changes the expression on his face to suit the atmosphere in the room Benjamin was slowly catching on and lucy was in a bad mood it was obvious to him however questioned she denied it and said that her mood was fine.

Lucy was actually right she was nice and calm puts her plants to wards Benjamin and this the Benjamin has to actually listen.

CHAPTER 14

With Benjamin in along conversation and agreeing
benjmain was to and agree that he would continue with
Lucy's experiment of going back in to his mind.
Benjamin walks out of Lucy's office

Starching his head and wanting tom known what
exactly he had agreed to. Lucy some how managed to
get him to re sign a new contract Benjamin was all
lucy's now and this time it ws even more un legal. Lucy
did not wait to tell Benjamin that a he had been
hypnotised in to signing himself back in to agreeing to
stay around and do the job.

However she was not keen on what his reaction will be
in the morning she agreed to pay him a again if he come
s back in one piece as he is going in to his mind alone it
was said on the contract that it would be a little
dangerous not just for Benjamin but for anybody else.

Benjamín is in the machine not knowing what to as for
what he is experiencing he closes his eyes after
watching the morning laughing as he looks at scene
after scene only to find himself all the way back to the
beginning. He was not sure if he had made a full circle.

However he was back in Lucy's office this short
journey that Benjamin was talking through his mind did
jot happen one or even twice but five times.

Benjamín was finally understanding and lucy the image
that was meant to be for her was not Lucy it was just
part of his imagination.
As for hologram who as putting Benjamin straight and
it took a hour to convince Benjamin exactly what he
was experiencing.

Lucy and Benjamin have a the ideas of why the things that are working of both of them. Benjamin is calculating there moments form the past. As Benjamin takes his mind their. Lucy was busy also believing that the microchip that Benjamin was recovering were the plans for the microchip.

Benjamin agreed that it had to be in that room somewhere Lucy disagrees telling Benjamin that a long time ago way back in the past you must changed something,
Benjamin thinks looking strong hand out everything including Lucy. As he continued and then agreed that he had got it all wrong.

Lucy gives Benjamin another conversation that he would never forget telling Benjamin at the end that she believes that the microchip is down stairs Lucy as she explains that the images that Benjamin sees through his mind makes sense.

He sees everything even himself and Lucy posting the envelope with microchip in to one of the lower apartment.

As Lucy had filled Benjamin in they move towards the down stairs towards the apartment both of them feeling excited as they approached the door. Benjamin is looking at it hard Lucy tells him not to knock as their was nobody living there and then lucy's tells Benjamin that the door is unlocked.

Benjamin looks at her both Lucy and Benjamin remove their weapons, creeping in slowly as if to expect some body there was nobody there.

The apartment was totally empty and Benjamin thinks that lucy had got it all wrong also until just before they leave. Exactly like the last time Benjamin notices the fire place and he walks over to it he is looking at it hard. The dead flowers over hanging the vase. dead.

Benjamin approaches the large old fire place again his nerves get the better of him this time he has a flash back another memory well infected but welcomed. Benjamin stands with his eyes closed he picks up the vase and the flowers of the floor in the fire place. Within the next few minutes Benjamin had found the microchip however it was well disguised about how it got there.

Well that would be another story Lucy I would rather discuss the future of the future.
No Benjamin knew what Lucy was going to do and then she asked she wanted to send him back just for the pleasure for the pleasure of Benjamin find the truth Benjamin again says no. Lucy smiles and apologises to Benjamin.
Lucy's hologram lucy switches her self off Benjamin is left to think about how he was going to bring himself back.

similar condition being imposed on the subsequent purchaser.

A CIP catalogue record for this title is available from the British Library.